Derail and Dispersed

Volume One

Stranded in the wilderness

Samuel J White

Enried / Twl

25/8/ 2024

CONTENTS

1

LEAD AUTHORS NOTE

On the night of the 22nd of December 1999, there was an incident involving a Norwich-bound train on the marsh between Great Yarmouth and Acle, in East Anglia. This book is made up of personal stories and eyewitness accounts of events in the build-up and aftermath of the incident. All accounts given are from employees of J&M Enterprises who were on the train that evening.

It has taken my friends and me twenty years to come together and write down our story. This is mainly due to the tenderness of the subject and the emotional state we find ourselves in as individuals.

In today's society, everyone wants to know every detail of everything that goes on, and then there has to be a tell-all book and a Hollywood movie for every tragedy, which is in itself a tragedy. For a long while I didn't want to do this, but as the years have gone by and circumstances change, those of us who have contributed feel we owe it to the memories of our lost friends to say what really happened that night.

Due to the length of our story and the huge operation of getting us all together in one place, we have decided to split it into a serial format and release it in parts when our busy lives allow. The incident was no ordinary rail disaster, and at the risk of us all being banged up in a mental hospital, this is our story.

Jessica Reynolds, Lead Author and co-founder of J&M Ent.

2

JESSICA PART 1

I've never been afraid of the dark. It's just an irrational human fear of not being able to see what's out there beyond the darkness. It's the things that use the darkness to hide that we should be scared of rather than darkness itself. As children, we imagine that there are witches, monsters and ghosts hiding out there in the darkness waiting to get us.

However, as adults, we see these fears as irrational and replace them with fear of muggers and rapists who hide in the shadows following their prey, or the burglars who use it as cover to break into your house while you're sleeping and steal your PlayStation or your TV. Of course, the ones we should really fear are the politicians and corporations robbing us in broad daylight and messing with our services such as the NHS to line their own pockets.

My name is Jessica as it says at the top, people call me Jessie, though I'm also known by several names including Sticky, a reference to my resemblance to a stick figure, and Sneezy, due to my chronic hay fever, but more recently I've been known by a different and more terrifying name.

"Muuuuuummmmmmmy!"

Back in 1999 I was, and I still am, the co-founder of J&M Enterprises along with my best friend from childhood Mandy Brown, but just because we owned the company that doesn't make us important.

The truth is we were just a couple of former factory girls who got made redundant. I went on to work in an insurance office while Mandy did three years of burger flipping before we both got laid off again.

After that, we took jobs with a so-called door-to-door sales company, but we quickly got fed up with the treatment we received from our boss and decided to branch out on our own. Armed with my GCSE in Business Studies. (Mandy didn't have one, because she did Home Economics instead.) That's the long and the short of it anyway, never for a minute did I think less than two years later we were going to be a well-established sales company employing twenty staff and earning more money than a modest girl like me, who was barely twenty-three, could ever want or need.

I was physically and mentally shattered. We were out selling six days a week to cover lost earnings over Christmas. That meant Mandy and me working three months without a day off. Mandy and I had been sharing a reasonably sized flat on Rouen Road just outside the new riverside complex in Norwich since we were two independent sixteen-year-old wantaways, and these days our living area was always full of paperwork.

Every night for the past week and a half that we'd been working in Great Yarmouth, at the end of each night, I'd gone to sit alone in the dark to gather my thoughts. I had taken a few moments at the end of each evening to chill out on my own, before going back to organise my team. On each of these times, I had gone to the end of the station as we waited for the train to come. Once there I'd take a few deep breaths and recompose myself, blow my nose, fix the little make-up I wore and take my inhaler if I needed to, as I watched the lights of the train weaving its way across the darkened marshland to meet us.

I would stare out into the blackness which runs for about ten square miles, mainly marshland crisscrossed by dykes. I would dream about all sorts of things hiding out there in that open space, the ghosts of any number of people who had died on the Acle straight over the years—(the road which runs across the marsh and is notorious for fatal accidents.)

Three years earlier, in 1996 a group of us had taken a drive out to the pleasure beach. It was a lovely day with family and friends. My brother Dave took his lovely, beautiful adrenaline-junky girlfriend Sarah on their motorbike and stayed later than the rest of us. Dave had hurt his arm, Sarah who was a nurse had bandaged it for him. Sarah (an accomplished rider) had taken charge of their Harley Davidson. They said they'd see us in the pub back in Norwich.

On their way down the Acle straight, minding their own business and obeying the speed limit, they were killed by a driver overtaking another car at over seventy miles an hour. What a waste of two lovely people. Dave, a mechanic was an excellent big brother to me, and Sarah was a great friend of all of ours long before they were a couple. They were very much in love. To make it worse, I found out after their tragic end that Sarah had been pregnant with their first child. They were twenty-three.

Surely, I thought if there were such things as ghosts, they would want to hang around those who loved them rather than stand in a dark field for the rest of eternity. I prefer to think of the inseparable Dave and Sarah drinking beer and riding motorbikes in heaven. Just to be clear although both liked a pint of beer, both of them were always sober on their motorcycle.

There wasn't really anything out there on that marsh, but the same sheep, cows and horses that had been there when we crossed earlier that day. But still, I was glad we had a nice warm train to take us back to Norwich, I wouldn't want to be stuck out there in the dark.

Obviously I'd known at that moment what was going to happen to our train, I would have pulled all twenty of my staff off of it and got them all taxis home at fifty quid a head. However, even that idea would have failed, because the Acle straight was shut for vital works. As I say I was shattered and run down having worked seven days a week for the last twelve and walking fifteen-plus miles on six of them—a hazard of being the boss.

The events of that night were put in motion way before we got on the train. It was just after 9 p.m., the cut-off point for knocking on doors, after which we would be breaking the law. We were slowly making our way back to the station. Mandy and I always walked around the outside of the area where our staff were operating, checking our friends and colleagues while making our own sales. We would meet in the middle around 9 p.m. and walk back to the station together. Mandy and I were both twenty-three and had known each other since we were little girls when she was adopted by a family who lived on our street, and we'd been best friends for twenty years at that point— (Now thirty-five plus years.)

At the time of the incident, we lived together in a small flat in Norwich where we ran our business. For a brief visual description, I'm about six foot tall and was painfully skinny, but not through lack of trying to gain weight. I have pale white skin with long dark hair, and I wear glasses. That night I wore a white winter coat over my blouse with a knee-length skirt and leggings with fake fur boots to keep my toes warm. Redhead Mandy, who wore a blue coat and trousers, is half a foot shorter than me, but without being rude to my best friend, she was quite big around the middle despite having lost nearly four stone—which I am proud of her for.

We were dragging wheeled cases to carry paperwork and both of us had our own shoulder bags. The streets we walked along were barely lit apart from the odd light escaping from under-drawn curtains. There was a frostiness to the air, which made me choke.

We were both struggling a little having worked nearly six weeks without a day off to make up for the group not getting holiday pay, which is one of the downsides of our job. Even though our staff were only given optional Saturdays in the build-up to Christmas, we ended up doing paperwork on Sundays during that time. Neither of us was feeling too well either, Mandy had a cough and I seemed to have been coming down with a cold all week, it was breaking out just in time to fall during our time off.

As we walked, I kept sneezing, blowing my nose into one of my large hankies as we walked hoping it would only be a short cold. At the end of a narrow street, we saw a solitary streetlamp under which we stood for a moment having a quick drink of water. As we were moving off there was a noise from the street which sounded like a sort of half cough half sneeze.

'Bless you again,' Mandy said nervously. 'That wasn't me this time' I sniffed. 'I was hoping you weren't going to say that.' She shivered. 'Why are you so nervous.' I smiled, 'It's just some poor sod out here going about their own business like us.'

A few moments later in the next street, we heard footsteps followed by the same half-cough, half-sneeze noise. Mandy froze; 'It could be a rapist waiting in the shadows to attack you,' she whispered.

'You watch far too many horror movies,' I told her breathlessly. 'Anyway, why only attack me? If they're going to rape you, they're not going to ask if you prefer men or women, are they?' Mandy is a lesbian and was in a relationship, but it was a secret as at that time she had only come out to very few people. 'My sexuality has nothing to do with it,' she groaned, 'In the movies they always kill the fat one and rape the pretty one.' 'But it's just us,' I told her. 'Your point being?' she asked. 'Well, I'm not pretty'

'I don't think many of the boys would agree with you,' she smirked with a little laugh, adding that most of the boys we knew fancied me, which in respect might well of been true, but I didn't like to think of myself as being physically attractive, because I put much more value into personality. She knew that I hated people who judge others by their looks and although I scrub up okay, I find it hard to accept compliments about my own appearance despite giving them to other people.

The chatter moved other things and a few streets had passed by, when I paused for a second to wipe my nose again. There it was again, The half cough half sneeze. Mandy froze and looked at me. I could- see her eyes shining with fright. 'Okay,' I said in my usual quiet calm non-panicking voice, as I was pretty sure there was no real danger, but it never hurts to make sure. 'Let's just walk as quick as we can until we're in a lit area. Just keep walking and don't look back.'

We had walked about two miles as fast as Mandy could walk, as although she was very fit for someone her size, she'd never been very fast. We were sweating like crazy by the time we reached the supermarket near the station. I took a seat outside the supermarket with our cases, Mandy popped inside to buy nicotine patches and gum. I was very proud of her for finally stopping her smoking habit, though my years of nagging her about it had little effect. I think I know who it was that got through to her. It was a certain young lady whom Mandy was having a not-so-secret relationship with.

She was only a few minutes, so I sat on a bench in the almost empty supermarket car park with our cases. The stillness of the place was quite eerie. When I gave my snotty nose a good hard blow into my hanky the sound echoed and bounced around the car park as though it were a cave. Suddenly there was that half-cough, half-sneeze sound again, this time it came from my left-hand side. I stood up and looked around, my heart pounding, but I couldn't see anything.

Then with an overwhelming panic, I realised the briefcases had been stolen along with our day's paperwork. I'm not going to go into the amounts we earn being in charge of the company, because that's not what it's about, but I need to say some of the paperwork in the cases belonged to our staff as well as us and we needed it to pay them, as well as ourselves.

I was in a blind panic looking everywhere but seeing nothing. Mandy came out of the supermarket and saw me standing there in a panic. She looked from me to the empty space where the cases had been, then back to me in horror. Suddenly, I saw two people about fifty metres away running with our cases. I pointed at them, and Mandy and I instinctively set off after them. Although I enjoy a good workout, sudden sprints in cold weather were not what the doctor ordered for an asthmatic with a heavy cold.

Somehow panting and wheezing I managed to catch up with the second runner—who clearly wasn't that fit if I could catch him—as they turned into a dark alley. His accomplice may however have been an Olympic sprinter as they ran off like Usain Bolt. The guy may have been unfit, but he was big and strong, and he grabbed me around the waist and held me in against him in one arm while he dragged my case in the other. Panicking as I gasped for breath, I heard Mandy scream from the end of the alley. 'What shall we do with them?' The guy who had me in his grasp asked his accomplice who had come back for Mandy.

His voice seemed vaguely familiar. 'Let's play with them,' he said, in a rather oddly high, yet again familiar voice. 'This case is worth a lot to you.' The heavy-set man who had me in his grip whispered in my ear.

I wasn't going to confront him, 'I'll give you a hundred pounds if you give it back now.' I told him in a terrified voice. 'Five hundred each and we have a deal,' he said. 'They're not worth anything like that even to us,' I replied almost laughing as if we would pay a grand for them when they were worth seven hundred pounds tops.' I felt myself being pushed forward into the car park. 'Look I'll pay up even if she won't' I heard Mandy shout nervously. 'It's okay, I'll pay,' I told her calmly, 'But there's something these idiots haven't figured out.'

'And what's that, my pretty?' Said the guy with his arm around me. 'Don't ever call me pretty for starters,' I told him, reaching in my pocket for my tin pencil case.

'You'll have to take us to a bank to get that kind of money, and even if there was a bank open at this time of night, I think you might get caught.'

'She has a point.' His accomplice called back. 'Okay,' he replied. 'Let's do it the way they do in the movies. kill the fat one, leave the pretty one to me.' With that, I took my tin pencil case and swung it at his head with a bang. As he yelped in pain, I slid out of his grasp and grabbed my case from him and ran. Up ahead I saw Mandy who was being held around the neck by a young man with chestnut hair, wearing a white coat and bright orange trousers, with a knee-length red skirt.

'Wait,' I thought to myself. 'A man in orange trousers and a red skirt?' Breathlessly walking over, I tapped the chestnut-headed person on the shoulder.

'Game's over Becks,' I grinned. She smiled letting go of Mandy. 'Got ya sweetie.' I have to explain that Becky—whatever she was she is one of our best friends and employees. She was well known for playing tricks on other staff and had been trying to get Mandy and me for a while now.

Now I knew it was Becky, I didn't need two guesses to work out who the man was. My tubby big brother Chris was making his way out of the alleyway rubbing his head which was sporting a big red bump saying, 'I think we can conclude that my skinny little sister can fight off thugs.' 'You're hardly a thug, you're a big fat pussy.' I teased.

Becky grabbed hold of Mandy and gave her a hug. Mandy however pushed her off. 'This is for scaring me bitch.' She took a swing at Becky and slapped her across the face, but it was more of a playful tap than an attempt to cause pain. She smiled and put her arms around her in a friendly hug. Just as they parted Becky turned and sneezed twice into the crook of her arm, with exactly the same half-cough half-sneeze sound that had been following us through the town.

'It was you guys following us through the town,' I grinned. Becky who had been wiping her nose with a rather brightly coloured hanky stopped and stared, looking a little concerned at me.

'What's up Becks?' Mandy asked her. She looked up at Chris and back to Becky. 'It wasn't us,' she said looking a little worried, 'We got here half an hour before you. We went and got food.' She nodded at two shopping bags against the wall to prove it.

'Becks thinks somebody was following us as well.' Chris told us, 'They're gone now though.' Becky added before sneezing again.

'Well, I'm off to the loo.' Mandy announced, 'Seeing as you two almost made me wet my knickers.' 'I'm coming with you,' Becky said quickly following and stuffing her bright hanky away as Mandy turned back towards the supermarket. 'Aren't you going too sis?' Chris asked me.

'No' I replied shaking my head. 'Don't girls always go to the toilet in threes?' 'Not this time.' 'I need to go though,' he pleaded. 'You go on the train.' I grinned nudging him in the direction of the station. I had my reasons for keeping him away. He didn't know about their fling and if you want something keeping private as they did, Chris is the last person you should tell.

As you can imagine, after all that there wasn't much time to chill out. I didn't get much of my chill-out time that evening anyway. I found Amber, who was one of my youngest staff, having her own private moment at the end of the station.

Amber wasn't everyone's cup of tea. A gobby teenager, she argued a lot with the other employees, but never with me or Mandy, although she gave us a lot of lip and cheek. She was trying to roll a cigarette, but she was crying so hard that her hands were shaking, and I had to help her, not that I condone smoking at all, although an individual's actions, should not affect friendship despite the fact I hate it.

I thought Amber had quit smoking, she was doing so well and was even going to the gym as well as working her socks off six days a week. Whatever was upsetting her had obviously kicked it off again. In fact, when Amber told me why she was crying, I'll admit I shed a few tears myself on her behalf, but I have no business talking about her problems and Amber has agreed to tell her version of events. It's up to her whether she tells you why she was crying.

We'd been having a little chat about things, and after I gave her a quick cuddle, she'd gone to the toilet to do her makeup, to hide the fact that she'd been crying. We agreed between us that if anyone asked why she was upset, she should say I'd yelled at her. Mandy yelled at people all the time, she had the bark of a pit bull terrier and the bite of a slug. Me on the other hand, I'm a lover, not a fighter. So, if I shout at you, you're in some serious shit as my own father found out when he made homophobic comments about my brother Chris. My bite is 'more like a venomous cobra bite, in the words of my late brother Dave.

One drawback of being the boss is that you can't take a sick day off unless you're on your deathbed. I felt like I was coming down with more than a cold. Joints burning, I was in dire need of a quick rest, before collecting the rest of the paperwork from the group as it was my turn.

I collapsed down on the first seat I came to, coughing heavily and smothering sneezes into a large spotted hanky, in a futile effort to avoid sharing my cold with everyone. I say futile because a lot of the group already had their own colds. After taking a drink of water I took my inhaler to help ease the tightness in my chest. Despite feeling so yucky, I was in a positive mood having had a good day for the most part. The train was alive with people, all of them from our group talking excitedly about their day.

I sat there, quietly smiling to myself as I listened to them all and thought about how grateful I was for their efforts. I was extremely proud of each and every one of them for turning from a bunch of misfits, myself and Mandy included—into the lovable bunch of almost professionals they had become. Suddenly, I felt a warm hand rubbing my back, which made me jump. I'd been so engrossed in watching everyone, I hadn't noticed my friend Sharon coming up to talk to me.

If not for my heavy cold, I probably would have smelt her perfume, which she used to cover up the smell of her rather serious smoking addiction. We all know at least one girl who is insecure about her looks, who plasters herself in makeup rather than accepting she's not a supermodel and embracing what she's born with—like I do. Sharron's one of those people. She's a lovely lady and I was looking for a kind way to tell her that less is more.

Twenty years later I'm still looking. 'Are you okay honeybun?' she asked quite loudly. I nodded blowing my nose loudly, yawning and stretching out my skinny arms. 'I'm shattered and full of cold but otherwise pretty good,' I told her with a weak smile as she handed me fifteen sheets of paper. Fifteen sales is more than I made that day, between Five and Ten is average, Fifteen is an employee of the month performance.

'Wow you've been busy.' I smiled, to which she teased, 'My mouth hurts from all the cock sucking I did to get them.' She made a repulsive gesture which caused me to laugh.

I didn't really believe that Sharon performed sex acts in return for sales, but she told everyone she did.

'How are you?' I asked, sitting up straight on the edge of the seat. 'I'm not so bad,' she sighed smiling, then taking a seat on the other side of the aisle. 'You on the other hand look like you need a holiday.' 'That's a lovely idea...' I sniffed, '...but top of my list is a warm bath, a cup of cocoa and bed.'

'I thought you were twenty-three on your last birthday, not eighty-three,' she joked giving my leg a little tug. 'I'd just like to go somewhere it's not flipping Christmas,' she sighed, 'If you're a single thirty-something with no kids, it's just a day to get drunk and wish you weren't a single thirty-something with no kids.' I did not mention the fact that Sharon had a daughter seventeen years earlier, who had been put into care because Sharon was a child in care herself at the time. I knew she wanted to find her daughter. Christmas must have been so hard for the poor woman.

Amber, who was her flatmate was the same age as Sharon's daughter, and I think Sharon saw her as a replacement at times. 'You know you're always welcome to join with us single twenty-somethings.' I smiled weakly, reaching into my bag to replace my grotty hanky with a clean one. 'We're only the next generation of single-thirty some-things-in-waiting. Although a holiday does seem a nice idea.'

'I came to ask if you'd seen Amber at all?' Sharon said, 'I'm worried about her.' As I said it was completely natural. Sharon and Amber were flatmates, and very close in a sort of mother-daughter way. I pointed her in the direction of the toilet.

'We just had a little chat about things, and she's gone to the loo,' I told her, being careful not to say that she was fixing her make-up to make it a little less obvious that she'd been crying.

Just as I said this, Amber appeared out of the toilet, looking a little better, but still in a bit of a state. 'What have you been up to now, Miss?' Sharon demanded of Amber. I was unsure whether I should step in. 'It's okay,' Amber told Sharon, regaining some of her usual swagger, sitting on the edge of her seat so that Sharon couldn't see her smiling at me.

'Princess Perfect was just giving me a verbal warning about my behaviour,' she told Sharon venomously, but she winked at me as she said it, telling me to play along.

'Well, someone needed to tell you, you were being a bitch sweetheart,' Sharon told her, putting a motherly arm around her shoulder across the table. 'You owe Jessie an apology.'

'I'm sorry I called you Princess Perfect.' Amber said mockingly, but the look on her face was serious as she offered her hand for me to shake, which I did. 'Now for all the other apologies you owe.'

'Yes Mum!' Amber told her, in the same mocking voice. 'Poor kid, I thought to myself as her friend Jack came walking up the train to join them, she moved over to the window seat so he could sit down.

As I've said, I never gave her a warning and she wasn't in any trouble. We hadn't been the closest of colleagues, or friends, prior to that day, but we were much closer every day since. Sharon was right though, Amber—who had joined us in the summer after leaving school—had been a mouthy little bitch recently, and some of her behaviour towards everyone had been very poor, but I knew why now. She was trying desperately to change her behaviour. All I saw was a teenage girl with a very rough past who was going through a horrible time—only some of which we knew about—and she needed us as friends right now.

I was almost run into by Becky who was bounding up and down the train like a Jack Russell after a ball, despite the fact she had a nasty cold just like me. I know this because she stayed over the previous night at the flat I shared with Mandy, and the poor thing had been coughing and sneezing all day but insisted on coming to work.

I love Becky. She had a classic case of undiagnosed ADHD and wasn't feeling well but couldn't sit down. For a proper description of her in the light, she had short chestnut hair, shaved at the back and sides, and spiked in the middle. Having taken off her coat, she was wearing a green shirt, with a blue tie and a long red skirt of her own making over orange trousers. A strange combination, but she pulled it off surprisingly well, like a walking rainbow.

'Mandy sent me to see you to make sure you're okay,' she grinned. 'I'm fine.' I told her warily, raising my hand to respond to her high-five request.

'I'll see you in a minute, darling,' she told me, turning on her heels and jogging back down the carriage, tripping on her dress and falling to her knees as she did, but she bounced back up and jogged straight on. 'I wish I had her energy?' Sharon told me, taking out three glasses for herself, Jack, and Amber. 'Don't we all' I smiled. Sharon took a bottle of wine from her bag which she had poured into three glasses.

She offered me one too, which I would have accepted if I hadn't offered to drive Jack home later as his mum was out at her work's Christmas party. Drinking on the train after work wasn't something I encouraged on a Wednesday night—although they usually got away with it at the end of the week—but as it was the last day before the holidays, I let it go. Technically we'd now knocked off work and it was their own time.

Sharon passed a glass to Jack, who from the look on his face thought she'd given him his Christmas present. Amber however took her glass and pushed it away and stared at it twisting it in her fingers. I looked over at Jack's left eye, which was a little blue where Amber had given him a right hook two days earlier when he wound her up. I don't condone violence, but Jack begged me not to take any action after Amber had apologised.

'I'm guessing you've made up?' I smiled; Jack looked at Amber. 'Of course, I've forgiven her,' he told me rubbing her shoulder. 'I can't not forgive her; we've been friends too long to fall out.'

She pushed his hand away and looked out of the window as the train pulled away from the station. 'You forgive too easily,' Amber told him, still looking out of the window not meeting his eyes.

'What?' he asked with a puzzled look. She took a deep sniff and came out with one of her twisted pearls of wisdom that I've become used to over the years, which only Amber could come out with.

'If you forgive me too easily, I'll just keep hurting you, and I Can't do that to someone I love.'

'You love me?' he asked clearly confused. 'Yeah, I do,' she replied softly. 'I just don't think a girl who hits you is good enough for you and that's why I said no to being your girlfriend, you deserve better.'

'But in your defence, I deserved it,' he told her. 'I was being quite horrible.' 'You were telling the truth,' Amber replied sharply as she took the glass of wine and swallowed it down in one go and went back to looking out of the window. 'I don't think I'll ever understand women,' Jack sighed.

Sharon gave me a mystified look. 'I don't get youngsters these days.' She smiled.

'I can see why you want a holiday' I chuckled. 'If either of these two ever qualifies as a defence lawyer, please remind me of this conversation before I consider hiring either of them.' Sharron grinned as I moved on to the seat where Kate and John sat arm-in-arm.

It was Kate's last day at work, for a while at least. she and John were having their first baby together and she was due any day now. Personally, I was amazed that Kate managed to keep working as long as she did.

Kate, who happened to be Becky's identical twin—although she did her best to be different. I.e., growing her hair and dying it brown—was nearest to the isle.

She struggled to stand up. 'Hey, you don't need to stand,' I told her.

'Yeah, I do,' she smiled and threw her arms around me, 'If you can't give your boss a hug on your last day, it's a sad state of affairs.'

'Okay,' I smiled returning the hug.

'Thanks for sticking with me' she whispered, 'I'm sorry for all the times I was such a shit, and you should have sacked me...'

'It's okay. You kept me on my toes,' I told her. 'Just stay in touch and I'll be the first one round for cuddles when little one's born.'

To be fair Kate had been a bit of a bad-girl rebel type. For a while, she was far worse than Amber. Sometimes she turned up for work bad-tempered, stinking of alcohol and cigarettes, and sometimes stoned off her head. In the past, she'd said mean things about Becky too. I'd never really seen them talk to each other, which was sad considering they were twins. Very oddly we hadn't employed them as a pair. Kate joined us from another company and Becky was Chris's friend. It was weeks before Kate had remarked in conversation about Becky being her identical twin.

I'd been very close to making her my first sacking for her attitude. Then I caught her snorting coke in a public toilet. It was then I realised she desperately needed helping not sacking.

I was so proud that she had grasped the offer of help in both hands. She gave herself the kick up the backside she'd needed, and she'd become a lovely young woman, I was sure that she and John were going to be amazing parents. I hoped she and Becky could make up over their differences, I was told they'd once been inseparable but sadly they barely seemed to acknowledge each other.

As I moved on there was a screech from the tracks below as the train began to shift, slowly at first, away from the station.

Next was a group of guys sat together, James, Greg, Charlie, and Michael. With the exception of Charlie who I'd known since I was about three years old, they were the charmers of the group. Cocky and overconfident, always creeping up to me as the boss—in a nice way. They were all boasting to each other about how much money they were earning. They always greeted me with wolf whistles in some alpha male type of joke, which I always played along with. They'd be over-complementary to me, and I'd hit them back with some witty comeback. It was all a game, harmless flirting, and banter. They knew I was in on the fun and wouldn't let them behave like that towards other women.

The clicking of the track beneath my feet became faster as I moved on to the next seat, where Irish Sammy and Spanish Sadie were sitting. Sammy was a large blonde girl from Belfast of about twenty-five, standing well over six feet. She had the loudest voice of anyone I know, while Sadie who came from a small town on the outskirts of Madrid (I will never know why she moved from the sun to cold wet Norfolk) was a more-reserved lady, like me. Sammy was flirting shamelessly with Tom the train conductor, who was about eighteen and went red with embarrassment. Even Sadie was looking distasteful and trying to distance herself from Sammy by talking to Rob who was showing her pictures of his young children.

'When you've finished embarrassing the poor boy, Sammy.' I told her, sitting down on the seat opposite. As I did so, I sneezed again and sat there wiping my nose as I waited for her to get her act together. 'It's like the land of the virgins around here,' Sammy boomed in her Northern Irish accent to nobody in particular but looking from Tom to me.

'I hope you weren't referring to either of us?' I grinned. 'I was talking about myself, Sadie, and Rachel,' she said mockingly. 'I'm sure you were.' I smiled back with the same sarcasm. Sammy was a known man-eater, Sadie had a steady boyfriend, and Rachel was the one person in the group who was happily married. Sammy stared at me for a second, and then asked, 'You're not the pretty tight virgin everyone thinks you are, are you?'

'You're right...' I told her as I stood '...I'm not pretty.' I wasn't a virgin either, but she didn't need to know that. I moved on to the penultimate table where our two oldest members Jimmy and Susan, who were in their sixties, sat opposite Carol. On the other side of the carriage, opposite Mandy, was Georgie our good friend who lived in the flat beneath Mandy and me.

A lot of people thought Georgie was a smaller version of me, but there were subtle differences. As well as being two inches shorter and having no legs, she didn't wear glasses, her hair was a shade darker and a foot shorter than mine, and she was much prettier than me. In hindsight, I think they meant our similar personalities, softly spoken, yet caring towards others, we also shared a very similar sense of humour.

Unlike me, Georgie had been through some really tough times, having lost most of her family in a tragic accident when she was nineteen. She lost both her legs and suffered mental damage in the accident and when we first met her, she had been a quiet introvert who didn't work or socialise and lived on disability allowance, which is her right as a disabled person, but it was only because other employers she had tried had favoured able-bodied people. In fact, we only met Georgie because she lived in the flat below us, and we found her trying to climb the stairs with her arms when the lift broke down. She'd been out shopping in her wheelchair without her prosthetic legs. Despite her problems, she had really come out of herself, and I've never seen anyone enjoying their work as much as she did.

She was friendly with everyone in the group, and we all adored her. I think most of the single guys in the group— and even some of the ones who were spoken for—would have given anything to be in a relationship with Georgie, but again, like me, she was happy to bide her time and stay single. As I reached her, I saw that she was knitting a set of baby clothes, which she had told me was for Kate and John's baby. When she saw me, she looked up and flashed a smile.

The train took a lurch to the left, and with a heavy bag on my shoulder, I was thrown sideways and was expecting my head to smash side-on into the seat when two strong arms grabbed hold of my shoulders and stopped me from falling. I spun around to see my saviour. I was amazed to see that Charlie had got out of his seat several meters away and jumped across James to stop me from falling.

'That was impressive Charlie,' I told him, catching my breath. 'No worries,' he said quietly. 'It helps that you're a stick insect.' He said gripping my waist, pretending he was going to tickle me before letting go. 'I was actually right behind you.' he smiled.

'Well not so impressive then,' I grinned 'But thank you anyway. You're still my Superman' I added teasingly. 'So why were you standing behind me, Charlie?' I grinned, 'I forgot something,' he said, reaching across the table where he picked up two empty cups from a fast-food outlet. 'I heard you guys were running late and it's cold and I know you guys can't function without coffee, so I got you some.' 'Three other people beat you too it,' called Mandy from behind, pointing at six cups on the table. 'And it'll be stone cold by now,' I smiled trying not to sound patronising. 'No shit, Sherlock,' he laughed 'I got them to put it in my Thermos flask.' 'That's good thinking Watson, bonus point,' I told him, returning the wink. I have no idea what the winking was for, but it's something we did.

'He's good,' said Mandy. 'Why didn't you think of that?' she said nudging Becky whose smile showed me that she'd done exactly the same thing. They'd both been so thoughtful I couldn't bring myself to tell him that I had the same idea myself. Then came another of my clumsy embarrassing moments I've become known for over the years. As I was thanking Charlie, that jangling in my nose started up again, I quickly raised my hanky back to my nose and stood there, wearing my stupid eyes-screwed-I'm-going-to-sneeze face for about ten horrifying seconds, before sneezing so hard that I lost my balance and fell straight into Charlie who grabbed me in his arms again. 'Bless you, mate,' he said calmly, giving my back a friendly rub.

'Oh gosh, I'm so sorry.' I said taking a step back. 'It's okay,' he mouthed. 'But I'm all yucky,' I told him, swaying slightly as the train sped up, and the clicking of the rails under our feet got faster accordingly, as I stood there wiping my nose thoughtfully. 'There's something else,' He smiled. 'What is it?' I asked, taking a big sniff, wondering what else he possibly had up his sleeve. I took the cups and put them on the table next to Georgie, who had heard our conversation and looked up from her knitting in interest to see what else Charlie had got. He turned back to the table and picked up a lovely bouquet of flowers.

'Wow they're lovely Charlie,' I gasped, completely stunned at the gesture, and in my haste, I gave him a big hug and a kiss on the cheek. 'They're for Mandy,' he grinned. 'Oh,' I said, suddenly feeling a little disappointed that they were not for me as I passed them to Mandy who mouthed a thank you. 'They're to stop her getting jealous when she sees I've got you these to say sorry for all the rubbish flirting, and for being such a great friend, and to say sorry for whatever I did that's making you avoid me recently.' He smiled awkwardly as he reached to the table behind him and pulled out the biggest bunch of roses I'd ever seen. I felt my eyes widen and I went bright red.

'Charlie, those are amazing,' I smiled. 'But I love our rubbish flirting. it's the highlight of my day, and… erm…' I didn't know how to finish as I put the roses on the table, and

Charlie passed me his flask of coffee and we stood there awkwardly both waiting for the other to speak.

Suddenly I felt Mandy's foot up my bum, shoving me towards Charlie, giving me all the encouragement I needed to step forward and give him a hug. 'I've been such a useless friend lately. I don't deserve you, Charlie.' I told him looking anywhere but in his eyes.

'I can assure you that every person here knows that's rubbish,' he replied putting his arm around my shoulders until I advised that he was probably getting too close. I was very nervous of people touching my person. Charlie was the only guy in the group who could get away with putting his arm around me, because I knew he was just being friendly. We had a lot of history together which I will let him explain further. He was the best friend of my late brother Dave, ever since we were very young. The long and short of it was we'd been in and out of each other's lives ever since we were kids, and I loved working with Charlie so much that this was the fourth job we'd done together. I loved the banter we had with each other, although I'd been avoiding him since he split with his girlfriend. I was slightly worried that I was starting to develop feelings now he was single and that could only end badly.

'No offence Jessie, but you look like shit girl,' he said awkwardly. 'I hope you're going to bed to rest as soon as you get home.' Before I could say anything, Mandy interrupted. 'She's taking a boyfriend out in her car.' 'What?' I asked. This was the first I heard about me having a boyfriend. Charlie's face, however, seemed to drop in surprise. It was then that Mandy reminded me I had offered to drive Jack home out in the sticks near Aylsham.

To be honest, Charlie was right, I thought to myself as I smothered another sneeze, I was feeling worse by the second and could happily have crawled into bed there and then, but I don't go back on my promises.

'I'll take him if you want to get some rest.' Charlie offered kindly until I reminded him, he didn't have a car. 'I could take your mini' he teased knowing how protective I was of my car. My 1992 pink Mini Cooper. It had belonged to Sarah my brother's partner, a gift from her long-lost father who didn't know she couldn't drive so she'd lent it to me and it was in my possession when she died. It was and still is my pride and joy, and nobody drives that car apart from me.

'You can come with me and make sure I get home okay and you can sleep on our sofa,' I told him. To my surprise, it was Georgie—who looked as ill as I felt and like me was wiping her nose after a sneeze—who put her hand up and waited patiently as though she was at school. When asked what was up, she came out with a question only she would dare to ask.

'Why are you two not a couple?' It was the matter-of-fact way that she said it that caught both of us by surprise. We both turned red with embarrassment, but I composed myself enough to answer without laughing. 'Georgie,' I grinned, although I was really talking to Charlie. 'I don't think Charlie wants to be my boyfriend, because if he did, he would have asked me out years ago, but I think he just wants a ride in my Mini.' I teased.

'I'm sure he'd love a ride on the back seat of your car,' Becky chirped in. The four of us girls all sniggered, which in hindsight was rather mean and out of character for all of us laughing at poor Charlie. 'Jessie wouldn't go out with me now she's a big important businesswoman.' he winked. 'Well, you don't know until you ask.' I replied a little tauntingly. He looked at me awkwardly and said, 'Would you like to go out tomorrow?' Unfortunately, I sneezed heavily again and shook my head as I was blowing my nose, to acknowledge that I'd heard him.

'I reckon tomorrow.' I sniffed.' I'll be at home in front of the TV with a big box of tissues.'

Before I could finish my sentence, Becky chimed in with a rather funny but ill-timed joke. 'Well, you'll both be doing the same thing only your tissues will be for your nose and his will be for his....' She shook her hand in the air.

Georgie who didn't get the joke looked bemused, as Chris, Mandy and Jimmy roared with laughter. I shouldn't have laughed but I didn't know he would take it the wrong way. Charlie, who had turned red as a beetroot looked down at the floor.

He turned on his heels and left me a bit stunned. I looked to Becky who was just as stunned clearly thinking that he'd take her masturbation joke as friendly banter.

Becky shrugged nervously standing up as she waited for my reaction. 'I think after that,' She sniffed sounding as ill as I felt. 'I may need to go and fuck myself....'

Jimmy was in stitches of laughter as were Mandy and Chris, but Sue who tapped Jim on the arm added sternly. 'Or you could stop your vulgar public behaviour and go and apologise to the young man.

I smiled at Becky knowing she had meant well. She didn't know Charlie the way I did and wasn't aware of how fragile he was.

I dropped my bags on the table and jogged with the little breath I had up the train after Charlie, I had just skipped around Tom the conductor when Charlie turned in surprise. 'Charlie hear me out,' I said breathlessly, with my cold and my chronic asthma affecting my aerobic fitness. I hadn't meant to brush him off at all, I just meant to say we had more to talk about and I didn't want to go out, because I really did feel like I was coming down with the flu. I didn't really know how a person is supposed to react when somebody who's been a close friend for many years had just got up the courage to ask me out.'

First of all, I had to confirm that he wasn't teasing me, then I muddled some plan in my head where I suggested that rather than going out, Charlie stayed over when we got home from dropping Jack off. Then tomorrow, we could have a duvet day or two while I got over this sudden illness with a hot water bottle and Lemsip and order in some pizza while we caught up on the soaps I'd been videoing for the past few weeks. (No sky plus in the 90's) while we talked about where we wanted things to go and whether us being together was the right thing after so many years of friendship. The truth be told I think the only reason we weren't together was because this was the first time in years that we'd both been single at the same time. I hate talking about my love life, but I'd be lying if I left this stuff out of the story.

However, Jessie often does things before she thinks and at the wrong time, and when I caught my breath a bit better, rather than talk I just flung my arms around Charlie. I'm sure we were about to kiss, when with no warning the lights went out plunging us into blackness.

There were shrieks of surprise from some of the people around us as a minor panic broke out. Without warning there was a loud bang from the front of the train, and I spun around to see a light flashing through a crack in the door, which led to the driver's cab. The screaming hum of the train's engines had disappeared. In fact, the train slowed down so suddenly that Charlie was thrown towards me hard and hit me side-on, knocking into me like a domino. Despite his best efforts to prevent me from falling for a second time, this time he was off balance, and I was helpless to avoid taking him down with me as my right elbow and the side of my face collided painfully with the side of the table. Charlie, although helpless on falling on me, was apologising profusely as I lay on the floor gasping in pain.

The train had come to a stop and there were screams from all around us. After a few seconds, a ball of light moved down the train towards us followed shortly by another. As I sat up and adjusted my glasses, I saw that the balls of light were Sharon and Amber holding their cigarette lighters so that people could see. 'I knew my chain-smoking would come in handy one day.' Sharon joked but suddenly all laughter had gone from her face as she turned a pale white and she began to scream incoherently. Sammy's high-pitched scream joined hers as I struggled up and Charlie put his arm around me and his hand over his mouth as though he was going to vomit. Warm liquid was spurting out of a dark mass, which lay a few feet behind me into a pool. In the centre of the pool was an oval-shaped object and as the light fell upon it, I was violently sick.

The warm liquid which I was covered in was blood, the dark mass was the body of Tom the conductor, and the oval shape was his disembodied head which had been sliced clean off as he fell against Sammy's seat.

3

AMBER PART 1

Hey, so I'm not a writer and I'll never claim to be, however, after all this time I've come to the conclusion that if this story is ever going to be told, it can't be complete without my bit, but my best buddies, Jessie, Mandy, and Georgie and the others, have persuaded me that it was okay to write about these things.

So, I've finally given in and agreed to put my story forward. My name on my birth certificate is actually Sophie Spellman. During my teenage years, a certain popular TV program about a teenage witch with my second name led the school piss takers to call me Sophie the Teenage Bitch.

So Amber is a name I fashioned myself in reference to a traffic light system, I am Amber because I don't know if I'm green or red. Happy or angry or both. So today I've joined the others at the pub in Great Yarmouth which my mum and I run together. I chose the venue because even before my mum and I took it over, it's the place where I have often come to chill out and reflect on the events.

It was me who persuaded Jessie and Mandy to buy the place and breathe some new life into it and my mum and I run it for them. There's something therapeutic about sitting at the outside tables and watching the sun rise and fall over the harbour. I used to bring my husband to that place and cling to him as I remember how lucky we are to be alive to see another day.

It's true irony that the day of the train crash was the day that I found that place. I was already having the worst day of my life even before the crash. I was in a horrible mood despite actually having made sixty pounds in my first hour at work. The pub was the perfect place for me to take a break. I ordered a large pot of coffee—enough for at least four people —and took it outside so I could be alone with my thoughts. With coffee in one hand and a cigarette in the other, I put my feet up on a chair and I watched the last rays of sunlight as it touched the choppy water of the docks.

Although I was huddled in my thick coat with the hood up there was something calming about the cold wind on my face and the clanging of boats bobbing on the tide and I wanted to be swallowed up into that moment. I sat there mulling over in my head the outcome of a consultation with my doctor that morning. I mentioned the place because it's somewhere I go when my depression hits me the way it did that night.

It was this same news I was mulling over that had sunk into me when Jessica found me at the end of the platform later that night, as she has mentioned already. By this time though I couldn't stop crying, my hands were shaking so much that Jessica had to light my cigarette for me, which was really kind considering she doesn't smoke herself— neither do I now. I took a couple of drags and put it out because it made her cough and she needed to use her inhaler. I didn't think Jessie even liked me (not many people did) and who would blame her if she didn't? I could be a horrible little cow when things were getting to me. I was in Mandy's half of the group, so technically Jessie wasn't even my boss. 'What's the matter darlin?' she asked me putting her arm around my shoulder. I was shaking so much I couldn't talk, but I was so desperate for human contact that I threw my arms around her and sobbed into her shoulder, while she rubbed my back and whispered in my ear. 'It's okay sweetheart.'

There were extremes of people I had met over the past weeks.

1: Those who had families who had money, buying big gifts for their spoilt kids, everything they asked for at Christmas. That was the kind of family I came from, apart from being the unwanted child who was lucky if I got anything.

2: The poor families who couldn't afford to spoil their kids but were more grounded family units and more appreciative of what they had. That was the kind of family I'd rather have had, just like the family of my childhood friend Jack, who always made me feel like one of them.

3: The families on middle income who moaned about it all. Why have a family if you're going to moan about it, when there are people who can't have kids who would gladly take them?

4: The fourth extreme was where I saw myself. Single lonely people who would give their left arm and probably their right as well to be in the position of any of the above. I hated it. I hated the whole god damn thing. To get bad news that day of all days was beyond devastating. I had always wanted my own family. At seventeen years old most people would laugh and say I had many years ahead of me for that. I'd promised myself I'd be a hundred times better than the woman who treated me like scum compared to my older siblings who treated me the same. My dad worked for Social Services so going to them was never going to be any good. It would later turn out that he was the bad guy in it all.

Every teenager has at some point shouted in a fit of anger, 'I wish I was adopted.' I didn't expect my mum to yell back at the top of her voice, 'YOU ARE.'

So, my dad had an inappropriate relationship with a teenage girl in his care and I was the result. I walked out of the house that day and I've never been back. Apart from Sharon, I had never told anyone this up to this point. I understand the reasons for what she put me through, but I will never forget, and I will certainly never forgive.

I set out to right all the wrongs bit by bit and find my real mum who was only a kid herself when she had me. I wanted to find a guy and settle down and get married and all that fairy-tale crap.

In fact, not just any guy, I wanted to marry my friend Jack. The trouble was he wasn't even my boyfriend) Fairy tales don't come true, not when you're seventeen years old and not had your first period. My parents never bothered to question it, and after leaving home at sixteen, it took me months to get up the courage to see a doctor. It was the worry over what they may find. That made me even more of a spiteful bitch than I'd been before. I tried to remain positive while I waited to see the consultant, I started jogging every day and eating more fruit, even tried to quit smoking. To be fair I hadn't done too badly having not smoked a cigarette in two months, which isn't easy when your flatmate smokes two packs a day or more. I fell off the wagon though, that morning when I got the news I'd been dreading.

The writing was already on the wall, but I think I could have taken it better if I'd been diagnosed with one of those horrible diseases that mean you have to spend thousands on

IVF treatment. I was different. Basically, I'd been kicked and beaten so hard when I was a small child that my ovaries didn't develop properly.

I told myself I was strong and that I could deal with it on my own. However, what tipped me over the edge was seeing families all at home together getting ready to celebrate Christmas and seeing John cuddling up to Kate with her huge bump looking like her baby may drop out, knowing that would never be me. Then there was Jack. He was my rock. The two of us had grown up in a small village where we were the only kids our age. Despite our fighting, we were very close and protective of each other, and I think that's why he gave up his place at college to come and work with me.

Speaking from experience, it's hard when a boy and girl who grew up so closely start to see each other differently as adults. It can turn a lovely friendship into a horrible thing, where one poor soul falls in love with the other, but the love is not returned. Jack made no secret of his feelings for me. I don't know why, I really wasn't anything to look at in my own opinion, and I wasn't even a nice person really to be around at that time.

I could be quite a happy playful young woman, but as I say, at that time, I was often bad-tempered and grumpy, yet Jack was never anything but nice to me. He had asked me out a few times and I'd wanted to say yes but ended up giving him a friendly cuddle and telling him I didn't see him in that way when I did but I didn't want to burden him with my shit.

I was always trying to get him to meet other girls in the hope that he would make someone happy. I think in a way it's the ultimate form of love, because to be honest with myself, it was because I actually loved him so much that I wanted him to find a girl who could make him happier than I could. However, I was hoping that when I got my results back from the doctor there would be good news and I could be the nice happy person I wanted to be, and next time he asked me out I would bite his hand off and say a million times yes.

But we know how that turned out, that was the last straw, the thing that tipped me over what I thought was the point of no return. I hadn't gone to the end of the platform that night to stare into the darkness and cry., if Jessie Hadn't found me, I'd be dead now. I would have thrown myself in front of the train and ended my miserable existence there and then and nobody would have remembered nasty little Amber. In some ways, I felt guilty that I didn't because in hindsight if I had, the only person to die that night would have been me.

So, that's the gist of what was going on in my head, and why I was sat there crying my eyes out and cuddling up to Jessie. She was an angel for helping me cover up the little episode. She didn't have to do that because she had enough on her plate and wasn't well either. The poor lady was coughing her guts up and sneezing into her hanky as we sat there chatting. Though I must say I was coming down with similar symptoms myself.

She had thought I was upset about my awkward relationship with Jack and was telling me about her own experience of young love. She was telling me that I should forget my worries and risk getting my heart broken, because if I didn't, I would always regret not knowing, adding that her failure to act on a young love when she was my age was the biggest regret of her life. She didn't say who the man was, but we all knew it was Charlie. However, when I opened up about the whole situation about my lack of ability to have children, poor Jessie actually cracked and began to cry herself. We had been there talking and cuddling so long that the train had already arrived and my opportunity to jump in front of it had gone.

I hid away in the toilet redoing my make-up after drying my tears and blowing my nose with a handkerchief kindly offered to me by Jessie (One of her many spares) when we were on the platform. However, when I came out, I went back into the whole acting like the cocky intimidating bitch that I'd been recently. She told me to be rude to her so that people would think she had been telling me off and it would save face from me admitting that I just fell apart. Even Sharon was fooled, and she was a good friend, we shared a flat at the time and she tried to be a positive influence on me and wasn't afraid to tell me when I was out of order. She would have made an amazing mother figure if she wasn't just as screwed up as I was. (No scratch that, she was far worse)

I hadn't changed my mind; I was just biding my time thinking of other ways to finish myself off. Something inside changed when those lights went out, it was like it turned on a switch inside When that train came thumping off of the tracks. I forgot about myself for just that moment in time, and all I could think about was doing what I could to help the people on that train. I ran up the train and started handing around the pack of cheap cigarette lighters I bought earlier in the day when I fell off the wagon and re-started the filthy habit.

Sharon stayed a little further back handing her collection of lighters out and laughing at the people who said she smoked too much. Had I known the fuel was leaking out of the train I would never have given them out. Jessie was lying on the floor being sick and looking rather dazed as though she'd hit her head, I could see in the light that her glasses were cracked as I passed her a lighter. I didn't realise that the stuff sticking to my shoes was blood from that poor young man who lost his head.

Mandy was struggling to bend down to help Georgie who had fallen under the seat. No offence to Mandy, but she's not the most agile at her size even with her weight loss. Being of smaller stature, I squeezed passed and got under the table to help Georgie. Her arm was caught under the seat, and she was face down in a warm liquid which seemed to be coffee, she was struggling to breathe as it ran into her mouth. She was rocking from side to side trying to free herself but her stumps where her legs had been were ineffective. I ducked down and got her on her side so she could breathe and helped her get back on the seat. I could hear Mandy becoming quite panicked at the other end of the train as they started counting people. I didn't realise why they were getting people off the train. I've always been taught that in the event of an accident, you should always stay with the vehicle even if it's a train. It wasn't until Georgie, who was struggling to speak, grabbed my arm, with Becky sprinting up the train screaming 'What the fuck are you doing hanging about?' that I turned and saw the end of the carriage engulfed in fire.

Quickly, coughing and spluttering in the smoke Becky and I helped Georgie to get onto the seat and tried to attach her legs but only one would screw in, so I carried the other one for her as she hobbled. I was waiting at the door while Mandy was organising things from the ground. John, Rob, Jack, and Charlie were helping lift people down. We helped Georgie to sit on the edge so they could lift her down, but as we did so Becky lost her footing and fell out of the door. Charlie did his best to try and catch her, but she slipped through his grasp and landed with a sickening crunch and a scream of terrible pain. She was hurt and I mean badly hurt.

Once Georgie was down, Mandy and I sat on the edge together and we were lifted down by Jack and Charlie. As I felt my feet touch the ground, I threw my arms around Charlie in gratitude and kissed him on the cheek. Jack and I took hold of Georgie from either side and helped her to hobble away. Becky was screaming and crying as John ran with her over his shoulder away from the train, which was now more than fifty per cent covered in flames.

In the light of the fire, I could see that Becky's leg was hanging limp having clearly been broken in the fall. It was an open fracture, and it was bleeding horribly to the point that I'm surprised the blood loss didn't kill her. Jessie was refusing to get off of the train saying that there was somebody still there on the train despite Charlie screaming at her to come down. Seconds after putting Becky down with the rest of the group we saw John running back to check the second carriage to check any other passengers, none of the rest of us had thought to do so, but Jack and I vowed to go back once we'd helped Georgie. We were about fifty metres from the train with our backs to it, when suddenly what I think was the fuel tank exploded. It was like being in one of those 3D action films with metal and glass zooming past our heads. Moments later we met with the rest of the group in a state of utter panic. We were in a dark damp field, maybe a hundred metres from the train.

Some of the girls were crying in shock, me included, and I'm sure some of the guys were too if they're honest with themselves. Georgie kept her arm on my shoulders leaning on me for support. Jack joined us as we went over to check on Becky. Sue, who was a former nurse, had laid her out on the ground with her good leg propped up on a briefcase to try and prevent her from going into shock. Kate, who rarely even seemed to speak to her twin sister, was holding her arm in one hand and supporting her unborn baby with the other as tears rolled down her face. Mandy came running over to Becky and took her other hand. There was a moment where there was a look of disgust between Kate and Mandy, but they just nodded to each other and concentrated on looking after Becky. At the time I was confused by it all, but I know now what it was all about and it's not my place to say.

I hadn't seen Jess or Charlie get off the train either, obviously, they did because they lived long enough to write this book, but I was terrified that we had lost them. Kate, who had been kneeling next to her sister stood up, her eyes searching the shadows for her fiancée. How she must have felt in the moment, none of us could have known. The man she adored, and the father of her unborn child had gone back to the train and was caught in the explosion.

Nobody said a word as she yelled into the darkness, 'You get back here...... Right Now!' She screamed, an echo rebounded across the marsh, then she put her hand on her baby bump and then in a tearful broken desperate voice, I heard her whisper, 'Please.' For a second nobody could look her in the eye, until she suddenly clutched her stomach and with a blood-curdling scream fell to the floor where several people ran to help her. 'I'll go and look for John and the others.' Jack told us. 'You girls stay here.'

With there being nothing, I could do to help in this situation I was best keeping away. Georgie thanked me again and I smiled and offered her a cigarette, forgetting she hated smoking. She declined obviously and I stepped away telling her I'd come and check on her in a minute.

I took a few steps back putting a cigarette in my mouth, and made my way over to where the other smokers including Sharon, Sammy, Mike, Ben and even Sadie)who didn't usually smoke) had congregated.

As I wandered over, I thought I heard a voice in the darkness say something to me and I spun around but there was nobody there just the wind. I saw Georgie a few feet away giving me a strange look as I turned back towards the other smokers, sparking up my cigarette as I went. It was as if she heard it too.

All of a sudden, I felt a pair of large hands on my back, and before I could scream, I'd been grabbed by something huge which whisked me away into the darkness.

Georgie 1

A strange meeting

Hey everyone, my name is Mary, but that's quite old-fashioned, so nobody calls me that. Georgie is a variation of my middle name Georgia. (My parents were posh) Jessie gave me the privilege of following her epilogue due to the relevance that my experience earlier in the day would have at the end of the night. But when Amber agreed to take part, we slotted her in front of me. My back story is long, so I'll tell you bits as I go along.

Be patient with me. Though I like to think I'm not disabled, I am, both physically and mentally so please be kind if my story is a bit hard to understand.

That was one hell of a strange night. I lost a close friend but found two more, one of whom I was to lose again almost as soon as I'd found them. The group was working the south of Great Yarmouth. My friend and work partner Jim and I, were on light walking, as were Kate and John due to Kate being so heavily pregnant. Jim's health wasn't the best due to his regular trips to the pub and smoking his pipe. Me on the other hand, I'm missing both legs above the knees. I did have prosthetic legs, but they were awkward things and I slipped earlier in the week and cracked one of the bleeding things, so I had resorted to swinging myself around on crutches, rather than being restricted by a wheelchair. No doubt I would have to wait for weeks before a new leg was ready, but hopefully, I would get a newer, more comfortable type. Also, it's not really fair to expect every house to have a wheelchair ramp so that I can push myself up to the door only to be told to 'Fuck off' by the occupier.

Some people would use a missing leg as a reason to sit at home in front of the TV, living off disability benefits and getting fat. I could have done that myself, but instead, my many health problems actually drove me to push myself harder.

I must have made for a rather lonely figure as I limped along the rows of houses huddled against the sea breeze in my thick trench coat. Jim was way ahead of me due to me having made more sales. I hoped to see him as I came into the next row of houses—we always waited for each other if one was behind—but he was nowhere to be seen. However, I had an inkling where he was when I saw a pub sign.

Jim often popped into the pub for a quick pint around teatime and I would sometimes pop in for a cup of tea to make sure he didn't stay for three or four. I took a look in the window and saw Jim sat at the bar with two of our colleagues, Sammy and Sadie. They all sat there with their drinks half-drunk, Jim sucking on his pipe while Sammy was slumped across the bar trying to light her cigarette while Sadie just looked bored.

I toyed with the idea of going in to join them, but the place was full of smoke, something that I really don't get on well with. Before any of them saw me I crept past and went on to the next house. This was a decision that would change the course of the night and possibly my whole future. The houses beyond the pub all had small front gardens with wooden gates and paving slab paths leading up to the front doors. There were no sales to be had in the first three or four houses. I was met with a polite no, and a not-so-polite go away and a no answer.

I sat on the garden wall of the third house and took a quick drink and blew my nose before I went on to the fourth house. I was unsure if I should knock. There were no lights on in the front of the house and there was an unkempt feel to the place, but it looked like there was a light on in the back, so it was worth a try. I hobbled up to the door and stood with my innocent-looking smile on my face leaning on my left crutch and raised my right hand to knock when the door suddenly flung open. I stood there like a bit of a lemon, (Like a lemon means stupid) with my hand in the air where the door knocker had been and my crutch hanging from my right elbow as I leaned on my left. In the dim light of the doorway stood a rather frail-looking old lady with a walking stick. she reminded me a little of the crazy cat lady from The Simpsons.

'Hello, dear.' She smiled kindly. 'Hi, I'm Georgie,' I said trying my best to twist the look of shock on my face back into something that looked a little more friendly as I reached out and offered her my hand.

'Ronda Fish.' she said taking my hand and giving it a limp shake. It was clear as my eyes adjusted to the light that she was a lot older than the fifty-year age limit of the health insurance I was selling. However, it was unkind not to at least ask her, and be shocked when she told me how old she was and pretend I thought she was thirty.

'Well, are you going to come in and tell me what you're selling?' She asked turning back into the house as if she was sure I was going to follow. 'Mrs Fish.' I protested following, 'I just need to tell you that I can only sell to people between sixteen and fifty.' She turned and smiled, 'My daughters are thirty-somethings. They might be interested.'

'Okay,' I smiled, nervously closing the door. It wasn't unheard of for someone to open the door before I knocked. Often people could see or hear you coming, but for someone to invite you in before you had even explained why you were there, now that's just strange. Even through my blocked nose, I could smell the damp mustiness of the house.

The hallway (which was poorly lit with original energy-saving light bulbs) took us past a rickety wooden staircase and a small kitchen before opening out into a living room. The living room was best described as cosy, it was not small but rather crowded with an old three-piece suite and a long dining table. Some may say the room was dirty and unkempt, but I prefer to say that it had an old tired and well-used charm to it. The wallpaper had clearly been there since the sixties, and the carpets and furnishings, despite being old and worn down were clean and tidy.

'I love your house, Mrs Fish.' I told her quietly as I took a second look around the room. I was not trying to charm her. I genuinely loved its homely feel. She turned and looked at me as if she had only just noticed that I was there. 'You sit down dear,' she told me, rather sharply pointing at a sofa at the centre of the three-piece suite. 'You girls have fun while I go and make us all a nice cup of tea.' 'Thank you.' I replied nervously placing my crutches down against the chair and looking around the room to see who she had been referring to when she said, 'You girls.' I suddenly realised that in my quick gaze around the room I had missed a young girl who was sat at the table eating a large plate of sausage and mash and watching the soap opera Neighbours on a large old TV.

'Hi, I'm Jenny.' she smiled. 'Be nice to our guest Lizzy,' Mrs Fish told her rather sternly. I was a little confused, but the girl calmly replied, 'I'm not Lizzy, Nanna.'

'Sorry, Alice.' Mrs Fish told her off-handedly returning down the hall towards the kitchen. 'I'm Jenny,' the girl said again through closed teeth, pointing at a seat opposite her at the table. Nervously I took the seat. To give an accurate description Jenny looked about twelve but could have been older maybe, was round-faced, with dirty-blonde hair and she was a little on the chubby side. It would have been rude to call her fat because that was inaccurate) Her eyes, which were looking right at me were so wide that they looked like they were going to pop out of her head.

'So,' she said in a quite hard gravelly tone as I sat down. 'You're a salesperson.' 'Yes, I am.' I replied softly. She stared at me piercingly with those big brown eyes. 'Sorry for wasting your time' she sniffed, 'Mum's gone out and Nanna forgot.' 'I see' I said smiling, but she just stared. 'You saw the state of my Nanna's mind,' she said without taking her gaze from me, which rather intimidated me if I'm honest because if there's one thing I'm not, it's a confrontational person. It had been quite clear to me from the onset that Mrs Fish was not of sound mind, and as I say, I could see she was outside the age range for the policy I was selling. I nodded and grinned awkwardly.

'You're not going to rip her off by selling her anything she doesn't need' she continued in her gravelly voice, almost as though she was threatening me not to take advantage of her grandmother's mental state.

To be fair if I had a grandmother in that state of health, I would have been just as defensive, but still, I tried to hold my ground and defuse any confrontation that might be had. 'Please don't think that I would do something like that,' I replied shaking my head without breaking eye contact. Jenny sat back and held her hands up apologetically, holding up her knife and fork with a large piece of sausage on the fork, then she turned away and coughed as if to clear her throat. 'I'm sorry, Georgie, I didn't mean it nastily,' She smiled speaking in a much softer, less gravelly voice tone. Her cold was making her sound like a gangster.

'Well, That's ok then.' I breathed. She put the sausage in her mouth and started to chew before deciding she had not said everything she wanted and raised her hand, swallowing the sausage before it was fully chewed, and causing herself to choke a little. 'I meant it as an observational statement' she said after a deep breath. 'Meaning exactly what you said that you wouldn't do that because you're a nice person.'

'It's okay to be wary,' I assured her. 'You don't know me. I could be anyone,' I sniffed. For the first time, she looked away from me and towards the TV in the corner.

'Did you notice that I know your name even though I haven't let you introduce yourself,' she added darkly. I stopped and thought back over our conversation. She had used my name but probably she just heard me introduce myself to her grandmother. 'I didn't hear you say it to Nanna cos I know that's what you're thinking. I know you better than you think,' she told me with an uneasy smile.

'Have we met before?' I asked her quietly. She frowned slightly and shook her head. As she did so I sneezed twice possibly three times into my hanky. 'Bless you, you are poorly.' Jenny said looking down the hallway at the kitchen door where her grandmother had gone. 'I'm really sorry if I pass you my cold.' I told her, feeling very embarrassed as I gave my nose a good blow.

'No worries,' she said with a deep sniff. 'I'm already full of it.' She added awkwardly, looking a bit distracted.

She stood up suddenly, leaving her dinner on the table. 'Come and sit on the sofa,' she told me with a sudden enthusiasm. I struggled up and hobbled after her and sat on the sofa at the centre of the ageing three-piece suite. Jenny sat opposite me, looking anxiously over her shoulder.

'Are you okay.' I asked, 'Oh yeah,' she replied brightly 'I just want to show you something and I would rather Nanna didn't see even if she is gone in the head.'

I was intrigued. What could a girl I'd barely met want to show me that was so secret that her nan had to be out of the way? She bent forward, took a tissue from a box on a nearby coffee table and blew her nose with a short sharp blast. Then she tossed the tissue into a bin, took both my hands in hers and leaned forward and looked me dead in the eyes.

'Your real name before you changed it was Mary Georgia Aricot,' She smiled. My jaw dropped suddenly. I was numb with shock. What the hell was going on. Nobody, and I mean nobody, knew my real name, not even Jess and Mandy, just me.

'That was what I wanted to show you,' she said quietly.

'You're a psychic?' I replied in an inquisitive state of shock. 'That is one way of putting it,' she replied softly, with a backward glance to the kitchen where her nan was still making tea. 'That's a really cool power to have,' I whispered. I was a little surprised when she shook her head.

'It's only one of the things I can do. In some ways I'd rather just be a normal teenager,' she sighed shaking her head. 'My dad left us because I'm a freak and my family want to hide my powers from the world in case people try to take advantage. They don't even let me go to school.'

'You're not a freak,' I said softly, knowing just what it's like to be shut away in the darkness, away from humanity albeit self-inflicted in my case. 'You didn't think that five minutes ago,' she smiled. 'True...' I nodded. '...but you have got me intrigued now.' She looked down at her knees and shook her head slowly and when she looked up, her eyes seemed to widen even more if that was possible as she practically beamed at me.

'Believe me,' she said softly. 'You have me equally intrigued.'

'I bet if I squeeze your hands a little, I can find out more about you than you know yourself,' she said with a grin, taking a tighter grip on my hands.

'Go for it.' I told her softly.

'You really are special,' she smiled. 'How am I special?' I asked in wonder. 'Well...' she said, 'For one, I felt your life force coming from seven streets away and I got Nanna to answer the door when you got close.'

'Really...' She nodded, 'You don't need to work, and yet you do it for the friendship and the experience of meeting new people, rather than for the money.' It was my turn to nod as she continued 'Although you work six days a week, (Unless Norwich City are playing at home) you also spend Sundays working in a soup kitchen for the homeless.'

'True again,' I told her. 'Told you,' she said with a rather twisted grin that looked somewhat like an evil smile. 'I know your deepest and darkest secrets now.'

'You know my big secret then?' 'I do,' she said softly putting her finger to her lips as if to indicate she wasn't going to do anything. 'And you don't think I'm mad.' I smiled weakly.

There was a moment where both of us looked at each other without saying a word, and then suddenly her face dropped. It was then I knew her powers were real for sure. There was a sadness in her eyes that told me she knew about the pain I'd been hiding from everyone.

'You poor lady,' she choked wiping her eyes with her sleeve and taking a deep breath. 'Three years and you don't remember anything before your accident.' I shook my head slowly and thought to myself how just for that moment, I wished I had just walked on to the next house and would never have met Jenny and her powers however sweet and kind-hearted her intentions were. I think I'd better explain that her powers were spot on.

Despite being born in 1977, my life as I know it started when I woke up from a coma in a Swiss hospital in 1996.

They told me I'd been on a skiing holiday when my family were involved in a horrific car accident. It's not visible when you look at me, but I hit my head so hard that I cracked my skull and woke up two months later in a head brace and my legs were obviously too bad to save. I was in the car with my twin sister and our little brother. On an icy mountain road near my grandparents' holiday home. My Parents and grandparents were in the car in front. I was told we hit them and slid, then rolled off of the road down the side of the mountain. That's bad enough on its own, but I didn't remember anything about life before that day and no matter how hard I tried I just couldn't remember anyone or anything including my family. If only I could ask my family what happened and let them help fill in the gaps in my memory, but that can't happen because everyone involved in the crash apart from me died at the scene.

Worst of all, I was found in the driver's seat of the car that caused the crash. Would everyone love me so much if they knew that poor kind sweet Georgie, who was making the best of her horrible situation and crippling disability, (Though no charges were ever brought) was actually responsible for the deaths of her whole family?

Would they look at me the same if they knew who I really was? Mary Georgina Aricot. My friends were my friends because they liked me for who I was as Georgie. As Georgie, I was just a simple disabled twenty-two-year-old, who was slowly recovering and seeing the world for the first time as though threw new eyes. She led a simple life and worshipped her friends. Mary the girl I was before I was me, was from a different world.

After months of rehab, I moved from our family home to my flat in Norwich and I took the pictures of my family and me from the walls and put them up in my little bedroom to try and jog my memory.

Still to me they were just dead people staring out of the past, even the ones of me. Because I didn't remember them, I didn't care so much about them, and I couldn't cry for them which made me hate myself even more. I stared down at the floor wondering if I should pick up my crutches and hop out of the door and get out of there before I got too upset.

On the other hand, Jenny's powers, however madly impossible it seemed may be the only way I could ever find out enough about my family to make my peace. Why should I have any right to use her powers for my own knowledge?

However, when I looked back, Mrs Fish stood beside the table with a tray full of cups and a teapot. Jenny gave me an apologetic look and removed her hands from mine. For some reason known only to her, Mrs Fish brought enough cups for five people, poured the tea for two of us as though she had forgotten, or just ignored poor Jenny. Jenny poured her own tea and went back to finish her sausages. Mrs Fish rambled on about the old days seeming to think I was an old friend of hers.

As I sat on the sofa sipping tea and agreeing with everything the nice old lady said, I felt my cold going downhill quicker than I thought possible. I must have sneezed six or seven times which embarrassed me a lot as it is not the done thing to go into someone's house and spread your germs, but each time Mrs Fish just touched my arm and said, 'Bless you, my dear.' I wasn't the only one as poor Jenny sat at the table sneezing badly too. It was almost as if there was something in the air that we were both allergic to.

Mrs Fish seemed to have forgotten about Jenny, but Jenny barely took her eyes off of me the whole time she sat at the table. I didn't know if it was because she was checking that I wasn't dying of boredom or if she was trying to read deeper into my mind as I sat there, intently listening to poor Mrs Fish. She kept repeating herself about her days as a fish wife on Yarmouth Seafront. Her tales would actually have interested me greatly if I could get my mind away from the insight I had into Jenny's powers, and the possibility that her extraordinary talent could help me fill in the missing gaps in my life if she would be kind enough. After finishing the second cup of tea I was running short on time and thinking I may well need the toilet. I hoped that if I made my excuses to leave, I might have one more chance to speak to Jenny before I left. It was Jenny, however, who brought a controlled end to proceedings.

'Come on Nanna.' she smiled 'I think Georgie has other people's stories to hear.' I stayed silent as Mrs Fish snapped suddenly at Jenny. 'It's rude to interrupt when the adults are talking, Erica.' 'It's Jenny,' she said a little louder. Mrs Fish seemed to snap back into herself for a moment, and finally looked at Jenny asking, 'When did you get here Jenny?' She smiled looking slightly confused, '…and who's your friend?' 'I'm Georgie,' I reminded her, and she smiled, 'Would you girls like a nice cup of tea?' 'We were just going out, Nanna.' Jenny told her, walking over and taking another tissue from the box on the table and wiping her nose. She nodded towards the door gesturing that it was time for me to go. She kindly passed me my crutches and offered to help me up and followed me down the long dark corridor to the front door, where she turned on a small light and grabbed my arm to stop me from leaving. 'Thank you for letting me read you,' she whispered, 'I am sorry we didn't have time to go deeper.' 'It's been a pleasure to meet you both.' I smiled.

She put a piece of paper in my hand. 'It's our phone number.' She whispered 'So you can call me if you want to meet up and try again, because it would be my pleasure to help you.' 'That's so kind,' I told her. 'Of course, I would love to.' I meant it sincerely rather than when I said it to all the sleazy guys who gave me their numbers.

As I reached for the door handle, she grabbed my arm and spoke in a more urgent whisper. In the brighter porch, I was stunned to see that Jenny looked somehow older, taller and prettier. Closer to my age in fact she looked a lot like my college Amber.

'You're getting the train home tonight.' I nodded 'I don't know exactly what's going on, but there's a ritual going on to celebrate the winter solstice out on the marshes. My mum's there, but I'm too young or they think I am. It's all innocent, but...' she paused 'But what sweetheart?' I asked concerned.

'I have a feeling that there are bad people too, and don't want you or any of your friends to get caught in it.' 'I'm sure we'll be fine my darling,' I reassured her as I stepped outside the door. 'I promise I'll phone you.' Jimmy was ambling down the street. He saw me and started to walk up the path to meet me, but Jenny grabbed my arm again.

'The spirits have a message for you...' she gasped with wide eyes. 'When the worlds clash, you shall meet your Grace and the key to your survival is the colour, Amber.' Before I could ask what she meant, Jimmy had reached us and Jenny seemingly spooked, backed away.

'I'll see you soon,' she said hurriedly shutting the door behind me. 'Thought you got lost,' Jimmy smiled.

'You know me Jim,' I grinned uneasily, going into the darkness with Jenny's message still processing in my mind. 'Make friends not money.'

'You make enough of both.' I couldn't see his face, but I could feel him smiling as he said it. He always told me, I was to him like the daughter or granddaughter that he and his deceased wife never got the chance to have. Just as he was to me like the dad or granddad I didn't remember ever having. If I had any idea that this would be the last time we'd walk the streets together, I would have told him my feelings more often. I didn't tell anyone about Jenny and her nanna, because I didn't know what to think myself. In fact, it quite scared me.

Jenny got everything else right, so when worlds collide, did that mean heaven and earth colliding at my death? And my Grace? Did that mean God? I wasn't even sure I believed in God. in fact, I had been sure I didn't until about an hour ago. The key to my survival is Amber, now that made me wonder if I was going to be locked in a cell with different coloured keys.

Then there was the other stuff she must have known about. Mary George Aricot, the person I was before I was me. Even though I was once her I didn't know her or relate to being her at all. Though I was me, deep down I was still her too.

She was one of two young women who looked at me out of the photograph which I kept in my wallet. Identical twins, tall, dark hair long legs hazel eyes dressed up like the supermodel their mother once was. They were in the fine clothes their rich father dressed them in, drinking champagne. Pictured on the front cover of a 1996 Sunday Times rich list. Mary and her twin sister Maggy Grace were the result of one of the world's richest men marrying a famous supermodel and having twins.

That was my secret. I didn't want my friends to know because they were Georgie's friends who loved her for who she was, and not because she was rich and well-connected. The real me, Mary Aricot after accidentally killing her family was now sole owner of the Aricot International Hotel Corporation.

My poor broken brain couldn't handle it. So though I retained ownership, I'd taken a step back. I left the company in the charge of the people in suits who are paid to do that sort of thing. I moved out of the family's multi-million-pound home, which I still own now along with lots of other rich person things like my dad's yacht. I found a small flat in Norwich away from the hustle and bustle and the press.

I wasn't prosecuted over my family's deaths because as I understand it, they didn't find evidence to prove that I'd done anything wrong. It was felt that my injuries and the loss of my family were punishment enough. That to me did not mean I didn't kill them. I kept the private family pictures on my bedroom wall. I wanted to remember them, I wanted to hurt and feel the pain of their loss. I couldn't be hurt over the loss of a family I didn't know and that made me a monster. I couldn't handle being that monster. So, I changed my surname and became known as Georgie Jones.

Nobody knew my secret not Jimmy, not even Jessie or Mandy. If it wasn't for the events that were about to occur, things would have stayed that way.

I remember watching with interest on the train as Charlie passed the flowers to Jessie and thinking why on earth are those two not together? They just seemed to me like they should be a couple. She was always inviting him over for dinner or for drinks or going to the cinema, but it was all because they were old friends. Forgive me if I was a bit out of touch, but I laughed at Becky's cruel joke about both watching movies with a box of tissues. I laughed because I didn't want her to realise, I didn't understand.

However, now I do understand, I'm not sure I would have been comfortable laughing if I'd known she was referring to Charlie watching porn. Strangely, Twenty-Two-year-old me, would have found the joke in poor taste. However, we must regress with age, because forty-two-year-old me would have pissed myself laughing. But that's not the point. I was looking back up the train as Jessie went after him and I was thinking, Go-girl, you go and get your man and tell him how you really feel, when suddenly, everything went dark, the brakes screaming and with my prosthetic legs lying on the seat next to me, I had no way of balancing myself, and fell backwards onto the seat, and slid under the table.

I lay on the floor with my arms flapping, trying to get up, but I was slipping and sliding in the cold coffee which had poured all over the floor from the extra cups that were bought for Jessie and Mandy. Soaking wet, face down and choking, I actually thought I was going to die, until my unlikely saviour and hero, Amber, climbed under and freed me. One of my legs had disappeared in the dark, but we managed to get one on and I will be ever thankful to Jack, Amber, Becky and whoever else helped. There was crying and screaming everywhere. After the blast that blew the windows out of the train there was the sound of crying and screaming all around.

Becky was on the floor with a broken leg, and next to her Kate was screaming for John who had been running back to the train to help the others as we passed. For all I knew Jessie was still on the train and so was Jimmy and maybe even John too. Jack also seemed to have run back to help as Amber and I stood breathing hard. I thanked her for saving me and she just smiled awkwardly, breathlessly saying. 'I need a fag. Do you want one?'

I shook my head and she called me a good girl as she turned to join the other smokers who were now all lighting up. I had just seen her light up when something grabbed her from behind so quickly that neither of us could scream. Without a moment to lose and with only my one false leg and my crutches on the soft wet ground in the dark I followed. So out of breath already I could not shout for help, I was following the glow of Amber's cigarette as it faded quickly, without a clue as to what in existence could have taken a full-grown woman out of thin air and carried her into the darkness. 'Bang' Something hit me on the head, and all was dark.

4

GEORGIE 1

Hey everyone, my name is Mary, but that's quite old-fashioned, so nobody calls me that. Georgie is a variation of my middle name Georgia. (My parents were posh) Jessie gave me the privilege of following her epilogue due to the relevance that my experience earlier in the day would have at the end of the night. But when Amber agreed to take part, we slotted her in front of me. My back story is long, so I'll tell you bits as I go along.

Be patient with me. Though I like to think I'm not disabled, I am, both physically and mentally so please be kind if my story is a bit hard to understand.

That was one hell of a strange night. I lost a close friend but found two more, one of whom I was to lose again almost as soon as I'd found them. The group was working the south of Great Yarmouth. My friend and work partner Jim and I, were on light walking, as were Kate and John due to Kate being so heavily pregnant. Jim's health wasn't the best due to his regular trips to the pub and smoking his pipe. Me on the other hand, I'm missing both legs above the knees. I did have prosthetic legs, but they were awkward things and I slipped earlier in the week and cracked one of the bleeding things, so I had resorted to swinging myself around on crutches, rather than being restricted by a wheelchair. No doubt I would have to wait for weeks before a new leg was ready, but hopefully, I would get a newer, more comfortable type. Also, it's not really fair to expect every house to have a wheelchair ramp so that I can push myself up to the door only to be told to 'Fuck off' by the occupier.

Some people would use a missing leg as a reason to sit at home in front of the TV, living off disability benefits and getting fat. I could have done that myself, but instead, my many health problems actually drove me to push myself harder.

I must have made for a rather lonely figure as I limped along the rows of houses huddled against the sea breeze in my thick trench coat. Jim was way ahead of me due to me having made more sales. I hoped to see him as I came into the next row of houses—we always waited for each other if one was behind—but he was nowhere to be seen. However, I had an inkling where he was when I saw a pub sign.

Jim often popped into the pub for a quick pint around teatime and I would sometimes pop in for a cup of tea to make sure he didn't stay for three or four. I took a look in the window and saw Jim sat at the bar with two of our colleagues, Sammy and Sadie. They all sat there with their drinks half-drunk, Jim sucking on his pipe while Sammy was slumped across the bar trying to light her cigarette while Sadie just looked bored.

I toyed with the idea of going in to join them, but the place was full of smoke, something that I really don't get on well with. Before any of them saw me I crept past and went on to the next house. This was a decision that would change the course of the night and possibly my whole future. The houses beyond the pub all had small front gardens with wooden gates and paving slab paths leading up to the front doors. There were no sales to be had in the first three or four houses. I was met with a polite no, and a not-so-polite go away and a no answer.

I sat on the garden wall of the third house and took a quick drink and blew my nose before I went on to the fourth house. I was unsure if I should knock. There were no lights on in the front of the house and there was an unkempt feel to the place, but it looked like there was a light on in the back, so it was worth a try. I hobbled up to the door and stood with my innocent-looking smile on my face leaning on my left crutch and raised my right hand to knock when the door suddenly flung open. I stood there like a bit of a lemon, (Like a lemon means stupid) with my hand in the air where the door knocker had been and my crutch hanging from my right elbow as I leaned on my left. In the dim light of the doorway stood a rather frail-looking old lady with a walking stick. she reminded me a little of the crazy cat lady from The Simpsons.

'Hello, dear.' She smiled kindly. 'Hi, I'm Georgie,' I said trying my best to twist the look of shock on my face back into something that looked a little more friendly as I reached out and offered her my hand.

'Ronda Fish.' she said taking my hand and giving it a limp shake. It was clear as my eyes adjusted to the light that she was a lot older than the fifty-year age limit of the health insurance I was selling. However, it was unkind not to at least ask her, and be shocked when she told me how old she was and pretend I thought she was thirty.

'Well, are you going to come in and tell me what you're selling?' She asked turning back into the house as if she was sure I was going to follow. 'Mrs Fish.' I protested following, 'I just need to tell you that I can only sell to people between sixteen and fifty.' She turned and smiled, 'My daughters are thirty-somethings. They might be interested.'

'Okay,' I smiled, nervously closing the door. It wasn't unheard of for someone to open the door before I knocked. Often people could see or hear you coming, but for someone to invite you in before you had even explained why you were there, now that's just strange. Even through my blocked nose I could smell the damp mustiness of the house.

The hallway (which was poorly lit with original energy-saving light bulbs) took us past a rickety wooden staircase and a small kitchen before opening out into a living room. The living room was best described as cosy, it was not small but rather crowded with an old three-piece suite and a long dining table. Some may say the room was dirty and unkempt, but I prefer to say that it had an old tired and well-used charm to it. The wallpaper had clearly been there since the sixties, and the carpets and furnishings, despite being old and worn down were clean and tidy.

'I love your house, Mrs Fish.' I told her quietly as I took a second look around the room. I was not trying to charm her. I genuinely loved its homely feel. She turned and looked at me as if she had only just noticed that I was there. 'You sit down dear,' she told me, rather sharply pointing at a sofa at the centre of the three-piece suite. 'You girls have fun while I go and make us all a nice cup of tea.' 'Thank you.' I replied nervously placing my crutches down against the chair and looking around the room to see who she had been referring to when she said, 'You girls.' I suddenly realised that in my quick gaze around the room I had missed a young girl who was sat at the table eating a large plate of sausage and mash and watching the soap opera Neighbours on a large old TV.

'Hi, I'm Jenny.' she smiled. 'Be nice to our guest Lizzy,' Mrs Fish told her rather sternly. I was a little confused, but the girl calmly replied, 'I'm not Lizzy, Nanna.'

'Sorry, Alice.' Mrs Fish told her off-handedly returning down the hall towards the kitchen. 'I'm Jenny,' the girl said again through closed teeth, pointing at a seat opposite her at the table. Nervously I took the seat. To give an accurate description Jenny looked about twelve but could have been older maybe, was round-faced, with dirty-blonde hair and she was a little on the chubby side. It would have been rude to call her fat because that was inaccurate) Her eyes, which were looking right at me were so wide that they looked like they were going to pop out of her head.

'So,' she said in a quite hard gravelly tone as I sat down. 'You're a salesperson.' 'Yes, I am.' I replied softly. She stared at me piercingly with those big brown eyes. 'Sorry for wasting your time' she sniffed, 'Mum's gone out and Nanna forgot.' 'I see' I said smiling, but she just stared. 'You saw the state of my Nanna's mind,' she said without taking her gaze from me, which rather intimidated me if I'm honest because if there's one thing I'm not, it's a confrontational person. It had been quite clear to me from the onset that Mrs Fish was not of sound mind, and as I say, I could see she was outside the age range for the policy I was selling. I nodded and grinned awkwardly.

'You're not going to rip her off by selling her anything she doesn't need' she continued in her gravelly voice, almost as though she was threatening me not to take advantage of her grandmother's mental state.

To be fair if I had a grandmother in that state of health, I would have been just as defensive, but still I tried to hold my ground and defuse any confrontation that might be had. 'Please don't think that I would do something like that,' I replied shaking my head without breaking eye contact. Jenny sat back and held her hands up apologetically, holding up her knife and fork with a large piece of sausage on the fork, then she turned away and coughed as if to clear her throat. 'I'm sorry, Georgie, I didn't mean it nastily,' She smiled speaking in a much softer, less gravelly voice tone. Her cold was making her sound like a gangster.

'Well, That's ok then.' I breathed. She put the sausage in her mouth and started to chew before deciding she had not said everything she wanted and raised her hand, swallowing the sausage before it was fully chewed, and causing herself to choke a little. 'I meant it as an observational statement' she said after a deep breath. 'Meaning exactly what you said that you wouldn't do that because you're a nice person.'

'It's okay to be wary,' I assured her. 'You don't know me. I could be anyone,' I sniffed. For the first time, she looked away from me and towards the TV in the corner.

'Did you notice that I know your name even though I haven't let you introduce yourself,' she added darkly. I stopped and thought back over our conversation. She had used my name but probably she just heard me introduce myself to her grandmother. 'I didn't hear you say it to Nanna cos I know that's what you're thinking. I know you better than you think,' she told me with an uneasy smile.

'Have we met before?' I asked her quietly. She frowned slightly and shook her head. As she did so I sneezed twice possibly three times into my hanky. 'Bless you, you are poorly.' Jenny said looking down the hallway at the kitchen door where her grandmother had gone. 'I'm really sorry if I pass you my cold.' I told her, feeling very embarrassed as I gave my nose a good blow.

'No worries,' she said with a deep sniff. 'I'm already full of it.' She added awkwardly, looking a bit distracted.

She stood up suddenly, leaving her dinner on the table. 'Come and sit on the sofa,' she told me with a sudden enthusiasm. I struggled up and hobbled after her and sat on the sofa at the centre of the ageing three-piece suite. Jenny sat opposite me, looking anxiously over her shoulder.

'Are you okay.' I asked, 'Oh yeah,' she replied brightly 'I just want to show you something and I would rather Nanna didn't see even if she is gone in the head.'

I was intrigued. What could a girl I'd barely met want to show me that was so secret that her nan had to be out of the way. She bent forward and took a tissue from a box on a nearby coffee table and blew her nose loudly. Then she put the tissue in the bin and took both my hands in hers and leaned forward and looked me dead in the eyes.

'Your real name before you changed it was Mary Georgia Aricot,' She smiled. My jaw dropped suddenly. I was numb with shock. What the hell was going on. Nobody, and I mean nobody, knew my real name, not even Jess and Mandy, just me.

'That was what I wanted to show you,' she said quietly.

'You're a psychic?' I replied in an inquisitive state of shock. 'That is one way of putting it,' she replied softly, with a backward glance to the kitchen where her nan was still making tea. 'That's a really cool power to have,' I whispered. I was a little surprised when she shook her head.

'It's only one of the things I can do. In some ways I'd rather just be a normal teenager,' she sighed shaking her head. 'My dad left us because I'm a freak and my family want to hide my powers from the world in case people try to take advantage. They don't even let me go to school.'

'You're not a freak,' I said softly, knowing just what it's like to be shut away in the darkness, away from humanity albeit self-inflicted in my case. 'You didn't think that five minutes ago,' she smiled. 'True…' I nodded. '…but you have got me intrigued now.' She looked down at her knees and shook her head slowly and when she looked up, her eyes seemed to widen even more if that was possible as she practically beamed at me.

'Believe me,' she said softly. 'You have me equally intrigued.'

'I bet if I squeeze your hands a little, I can find out more about you than you know yourself,' she said with a grin, taking a tighter grip on my hands.

'Go for it.' I told her softly.

'You really are special,' she smiled. 'How am I special?' I asked in wonder. 'Well...' she said, 'For one, I felt your life force coming from seven streets away and I got Nanna to answer the door when you got close.'

'Really...' She nodded, 'You don't need to work, and yet you do it for the friendship and the experience of meeting new people, rather than for the money.' It was my turn to nod as she continued 'Although you work six days a week, (Unless Norwich city are playing at home) you also spend Sundays working in a soup kitchen for the homeless.'

'True again,' I told her. 'Told you,' she said with a rather twisted grin that looked somewhat like an evil smile. 'I know your deepest and darkest secrets now.'

'You know my big secret then?' 'I do,' she said softly putting her finger to her lips as if to indicate she wasn't going to do anything. 'And you don't think I'm mad.' I smiled weakly.

There was a moment where both of us looked at each other without saying a word, and then suddenly her face dropped. It was then I knew her powers were real for sure. There was a sadness in her eyes that told me she knew about the pain I'd been hiding from everyone.

'You poor lady,' she choked wiping her eyes with her sleeve and taking a deep breath. 'Three years and you don't remember anything before your accident.' I shook my head slowly and thought to myself how just for that moment, I wished I had just walked on to the next house and would never have met Jenny and her powers however sweet and kind-hearted her intentions were. I think I'd better explain that her powers were spot on. Despite being born in 1977, my life as I know it started when I woke up from a coma in a Swiss hospital in 1996.

They told me I'd been on a skiing holiday when my family were involved in a horrific car accident. It's not visible when you look at me, but I hit my head so hard that I cracked my skull and woke up two months later in a head brace and my legs were obviously too bad to save. I was in the car with my twin sister and our little brother. On an icy mountain road near my grandparents' holiday home. My Parents and grandparents were in the car in front. I was told we hit them and slid, then rolled off of the road down the side of the mountain. That's bad enough on its own, but I didn't remember anything about life before that day and no matter how hard I tried I just couldn't remember anyone or anything including my family. If only I could ask my family what happened and let them help fill in the gaps in my memory, but that can't happen because everyone involved in the crash apart from me died at the scene.

Worst of all, I was found in the driver's seat of the car that caused the crash. Would everyone love me so much if they knew that poor kind sweet Georgie, who was making the best of her horrible situation and crippling disability, (Though no charges were ever brought) was actually responsible for the deaths of her whole family?

Would they look at me the same if they knew who I really was. Mary Georgina Aricot. My friends were my friends because they liked me for who I was as Georgie. As Georgie, I was just a simple disabled twenty-two-year-old, who was slowly recovering and seeing the world for the first time as though threw new eyes. She led a simple life and worshipped her friends. Mary the girl I was before I was me, was from a different world.

After months of rehab, I moved from our family home to my flat in Norwich and I took the pictures of my family and me from the walls and put them up in my little bedroom to try and jog my memory.

Still to me they were just dead people staring out of the past, even the ones of me. Because I didn't remember them, I didn't care so much about them, and I couldn't cry for them which made me hate myself even more. I stared down at the floor wondering if I should pick up my crutches and hop out of the door and get out of there before I got too upset.

On the other hand, Jenny's powers, however madly impossible it seemed may be the only way I could ever find out enough about my family to make my peace. Although why should I have any right to use her powers for my own knowledge?

However, when I looked back, Mrs Fish stood beside the table with a tray full of cups and a teapot. Jenny gave me an apologetic look and removed her hands from mine. For some reason known only to her, Mrs Fish brought enough cups for five people, poured the tea for two of us as though she had forgotten, or just ignored poor Jenny. Jenny poured her own tea and went back to finish her sausages. Mrs Fish rambled on about the old days seeming to think I was an old friend of hers.

As I sat on the sofa sipping tea and agreeing with everything the nice old lady said, I felt my cold going downhill quicker than I thought possible. I must have sneezed six or seven times which embarrassed me a lot as it is not the done thing to go into someone's house and spread your germs, but each time Mrs Fish just touched my arm and said, 'Bless you my dear.' I wasn't the only one as poor Jenny sat at the table sneezing badly too. It was almost as if there was something in the air that we were both allergic to.

Mrs Fish seemed to have forgotten about Jenny, but Jenny barely took her eyes off of me the whole time she sat at the table. I didn't know if it was because she was checking that I wasn't dying of boredom or if she was trying to read deeper into my mind as I sat there, intently listening to poor Mrs Fish. She kept repeating herself about her days as a fish wife on Yarmouth Seafront. Her tales would actually have interested me greatly if I could get my mind away from the insight I had into Jenny's powers, and the possibility that her extraordinary talent could help me fill in the missing gaps in my life if she would be kind enough. After finishing the second cup of tea I was running short on time and thinking I may well need the toilet. I hoped that if I made my excuses to leave, I might have one more chance to speak to Jenny before I left. It was Jenny, however, who brought a controlled end to proceedings.

'Come on Nanna.' she smiled 'I think Georgie has other people's stories to hear.' I stayed silent as Mrs Fish snapped suddenly at Jenny. 'It's rude to interrupt when the adults are talking, Erica.' 'It's Jenny,' she said a little louder. Mrs Fish seemed to snap back into herself for a moment, and finally looked at Jenny asking, 'When did you get here Jenny?' She smiled looking slightly confused, '...and who's your friend?' 'I'm Georgie,' I reminded her, and she smiled, 'Would you girls like a nice cup of tea?' 'We were just going out, Nanna.' Jenny told her, walking over and taking another tissue from the box on the table and wiping her nose. She nodded towards the door gesturing that it was time for me to go. She kindly passed me my crutches and offered to help me up and followed me down the long dark corridor to the front door, where she turned on a small light and grabbed my arm to stop me from leaving. 'Thank you for letting me read you,' she whispered, 'I am sorry we didn't have time to go deeper.' 'It's been a pleasure to meet you both.' I smiled.

She put a piece of paper in my hand. 'It's our phone number.' She whispered 'So you can call me if you want to meet up and try again, because it would be my pleasure to help you.' 'That's so kind,' I told her. 'Of course, I would love to.' I meant it sincerely rather than when I said it to all the sleazy guys who gave me their numbers.

As I reached for the door handle, she grabbed my arm and spoke in a more urgent whisper. In the brighter porch, I was stunned to see that Jenny looked somehow older. Closer to my age in fact she looked a lot like my college Amber.

'You're getting the train home tonight.' I nodded 'I don't know exactly what's going on, but there's a ritual going on to celebrate the winter solstice out on the marshes. My mum's there, but I'm too young or they think I am. It's all innocent, but...' she paused 'But what sweetheart?' I asked concerned.

'I have a feeling that there are bad people too, and don't want you or any of your friends to get caught in it.' 'I'm sure we'll be fine my darling,' I reassured her as I stepped outside the door. 'I promise I'll phone you.' Jimmy was ambling down the street. He saw me and started to walk up the path to meet me, but Jenny grabbed my arm again.

'The spirits have a message for you...' she gasped with wide eyes. 'When the worlds clash, you shall meet your Grace and the key to your survival is the colour, Amber.' Before I could ask what she meant, Jimmy had reached us and Jenny seemingly spooked, backed away.

'I'll see you soon,' she said hurriedly shutting the door behind me. 'Thought you got lost,' Jimmy smiled.

'You know me Jim,' I grinned uneasily, going into the darkness with Jenny's message still processing in my mind. 'Make friends not money.'

'You make enough of both.' I couldn't see his face, but I could feel him smiling as he said it. He always told me, I was to him like the daughter or granddaughter that he and his deceased wife never got the chance to have. Just as he was to me like the dad or granddad I didn't remember ever having. If I had any idea that this would be the last time we'd walk the streets together, I would have told him my feelings more often. I didn't tell anyone about Jenny and her nanna, because I didn't know what to think myself. In fact, it quite scared me.

Jenny got everything else right, so when worlds collide, did that mean heaven and earth colliding at my death? And my Grace? Did that mean God? I wasn't even sure I believed in God. in fact, I had been sure I didn't until about an hour ago. The key to my survival is Amber, now that made me wonder if I was going to be locked in a cell with different coloured keys.

Then there was the other stuff she must have known about. Mary George Aricot, the person I was before I was me. Even though I was once her I didn't know her or relate to being her at all. Though I was me, deep down I was still her too.

She was one of two young women who looked at me out of the photograph which I kept in my wallet. Identical twins, tall, dark hair long legs hazel eyes dressed up like the supermodel their mother once was. They were in the fine clothes their rich father dressed them in, drinking champagne. Pictured on the front cover off a 1996 Sunday time's rich list. Mary and her twin sister Maggy Grace were the result of one of the world's richest men marrying a famous supermodel and having twins.

That was my secret. I didn't want my friends to know because they were Georgie's friends who loved her for who she was, and not because she was rich and well-connected. The real me, Mary Aricot after accidentally killing her family was now sole owner of the Aricot International Hotel Corporation.

My poor broken brain couldn't handle it. So though I retained ownership, I'd taken a step back. I left the company in the charge of the people in suits who are paid to do that sort of thing. I moved out of the family's multi-million-pound home, which I still own now and along with lots of other rich person things like my dad's yacht. I found a small flat in Norwich away from the hustle and bustle and the press.

I wasn't prosecuted over my family's deaths because as I understand it, they didn't find evidence to prove that I done anything wrong. It was felt that my injuries and the loss of my family were punishment enough. That to me did not mean I didn't kill them. I kept the private family pictures on my bedroom wall. I wanted to remember them, I wanted to hurt and feel the pain of their loss. I couldn't hurt over the loss of a family I didn't know and that made me a monster. I couldn't handle being that monster. So, I changed my surname and became known as Georgie Jones.

Nobody knew my secret not Jimmy, not even Jessie or Mandy. If it wasn't for the events that were about to occur, things would have stayed that way.

I remember watching with interest on the train as Charlie passed the flowers to Jessie and thinking why on earth are those two not together. They just seemed to me like they should be a couple. She was always inviting him over for dinner or for drinks or going to the cinema, but it was all because they were old friends. Forgive me if I was a bit out of touch, but I laughed at Becky's cruel joke about both watching movies with a box of tissues. I laughed because I didn't want her to realise, I didn't understand.

However, now I do understand, I'm not sure I would have been comfortable laughing if I'd known she was referring to Charlie watching porn. Strangely, Twenty-Two-year-old me, would have found the joke in poor taste. However, we must regress with age, because forty-two-year-old me would have pissed myself laughing. But that's not the point. I was looking back up the train as Jessie went after him and I was thinking, Go-girl, you go and get your man and tell him how you really feel, when suddenly, everything went dark, the brakes screaming and with my prosthetic legs lying on the seat next to me, I had no way of balancing myself, and fell backwards onto the seat, and slid under the table.

I laid on the floor with my arms flapping, trying to get up, but I was slipping and sliding in the cold coffee which had poured all over the floor from the extra cups that were bought for Jessie and Mandy. Soaking wet, face down and choking, I actually thought I was going to die, until my unlikely saviour and hero, Amber, climbed under and freed me. One of my legs had disappeared in the dark, but we managed to get one on and I will be ever thankful to Jack, Amber, Becky and whoever else helped. There was crying and screaming everywhere. After the blast that blew the windows out of the train, there was the sound of crying and screaming all around.

Becky was on the floor with a broken leg, and next to her Kate was screaming for John who had been running back to the train to help the others as we passed. For all I knew Jessie was still on the train and so was Jimmy and maybe even John too. Jack also seemed to have run back to help as Amber and I stood breathing hard. I thanked her for saving me and she just smiled awkwardly, breathlessly saying. 'I need a fag. Do you want one?'

I shook my head and she called me a good girl as she turned to join the other smokers who were now all lighting up. I had just seen her light up when something grabbed her from behind so quickly that neither of us could scream. Without a moment to lose and with only my one false leg and my crutches on the soft wet ground in the dark I followed. So out of breath already I could not shout for help, I was following the glow of Amber's cigarette as it faded quickly, without a clue as to what in existence could have taken a full-grown woman out of thin air and carried her into the darkness. 'Bang' Something hit me on the head, and all was dark.

5

CHARLIE 1

There were many places I could have been that night when the train came off the rails, but in a rather morbid way, given the other choices, I wouldn't have changed a thing. If I hadn't been there at work that night, the alternative for me would have been to sit at home, watching TV on an empty sofa, before laying in a cold empty bed which I used to share with my girlfriend of two years until she inexplicably left me. I think in some twisted way we were all fated to be on that train. When I look back and go over things, I see a pattern which suggests my whole life had been somehow manipulated towards me being there.

In truth, fate always seemed to bring me back to Jessica and she was my cast iron reason for being there. Admittedly my reputation as a charmer, and the fact that I bought her flowers, might have seemed to the others as though I was either being a blatant suck-up to the boss or that I chose a really bad time to ask her out. However, the real reason that I bought her the flowers was that I'd seen her struggling over the past few days and wanted to do something to show my appreciation for her hard work and friendship.

To be clear, even though I cared really deeply for her, I had no intention of asking her out until she invited me. Even when Becky joked about me wanking it didn't embarrass me it was funny, but I just felt it was time to leave the ladies to it.

I just thought it was banter amongst friends, and when I walked off, I didn't think Jessie was saying no to a relationship with me. I never thought such a thing was on the cards. I was just going back to my seat. My insistence on going with her to take Jack home wasn't me trying to hit on her. I was generally concerned about my friend. She and Mandy had run themselves into the ground for that business.

In the last couple of years, they had walked miles and miles and got little sleep. Mandy was looking tired, better for the extra exercise, but Jessie was always a slim and very fit girl, she loved her swimming, but despite her eating well, she was looking drained from all the extra walking. Jessie and Mandy being in charge had to do more walking than the rest of us. Jessie still had that mischievous spark in her eyes, but the bags around them were concerning me. Somehow, Jessie and I had always been close in one way or another. I had known her since she was about three. We'd grown up on the same street in Mile Cross and she was the little sister of my best mate Dave.

Their mother was a childminder. After my mum passed away when I was five I'd go to their house after school so my old man god rest his soul could bust a gut to keep a roof over our heads. I'm pretty sure their mum only charged him for food. Dave and I would often hang out with a boy called Max whose parents adopted Mandy, and as we got a little older, we used to play out in the streets in the summer with a lot of other kids, including my neighbour Sarah, who as Jessie explained was Killed along with Dave three years earlier.

It was the eighties and parents were not paranoid about their children, like nowadays, and with no kids' TV channels, or iPads, internet, or any of that crap, we stayed out until the streetlamps came on, playing in the park. Dave and Max may have moaned about their sisters, but I found their presence very welcome. Mandy was just a huge laugh —in size and personality) and Jessie especially, was an intelligent engaging girl. Jessie had five brothers, but she clung to Dave because he was closest in age, but though he worshipped his little sister, he'd ask me to keep an eye on her sometimes. I am sure he didn't mean until she was twenty-three. In fact, I have fond memories of helping Jessie learn to swim one summer in the fenced-off stretch of river at Wensum Park where most of the poor kids in Norwich went.

Of course, things changed as the eighties came to a close. I finished with school and started work with my old man at the sweet factory, and Dave became a mechanic's apprentice. Time for socialising was limited to me. Dave and I and a few other guys often went to drink in whichever of the local watering holes didn't care that we were underage. Jessie moved in with her much older brother and his partner when she was twelve after a blazing row with her father. Dave who really did care about his sister would meet her at our house as he couldn't go to her house. Sometimes in fact, always she would get there early and have a cup of tea with me before spending time with him.

In 1990 she and Mandy got jobs in the sweet factory in the city where I was working. That's how Mandy got fat because she ate a lot of the produce. I think the problem was that there was always an underlying connection between Jessie and I.

However, there is an unwritten rule between friends that you don't ask out your best friend's little sister if you want to remain friends. Despite this, we had all remained a very tight group and we'd all go out drinking down the local pub after work. However, Jess, Mandy, myself, and my old man were all laid off in the early part of 1994, and with the loss of nine hundred jobs which would devastate the city for many years to come.

I was lucky enough to get a job at Norwich Union Insurance. I had been there a couple of weeks when I was sat at my desk at the call centre one morning when someone put their hands over my eyes and whispered in my ear, 'Guess who Charlie.' I couldn't forget that voice. Jessie had got a job as a general office body, tea making photocopying that sort of thing. We'd often have lunch together. We worked there a good three and a half years, in which time we got the horrible news that Dave and Sarah had been killed in a motorcycle accident. Maybe it was just because she was with me having a drink in the pub with me and my then girlfriend when we got the news, or because she was fighting her parents and didn't go to them. It was me who sat there in shock, cuddling her all night, and my shoulder she cried on at the funeral, ignoring her parents altogether apart from a brief hug with her mum and two-fingered salutes to her father.

My friendship with Jessie remained strong, but by the time I was twenty-one and she was nineteen, I began to realise that our close friendship wasn't going to blossom into anything else. That was when I started seeing a girl, Joanne, or Smokey Jo as we called her. The only downside for Smokey Jo was the reason for her nickname, she could rarely be found without a cigarette on the go, and I don't smoke, but despite this, I thought Jo was the love for me.

Jo, Jessie, and Mandy were all in the same year at school and all friends, so all was well for a few years, apart from my dear old man, who never got over the loss of my mum, He died from drinking and smoking-related problems in 1995.

Then again, Jessie and I were given a few months' notice that our jobs were being cut, and within a few days she was gone from work, and although I saw her socially, she kept tight-lipped about what she was doing for employment, until she called me one day, knowing my job was coming to an end and told me about her new business venture.

That was when I started working for J.A.M. I watched proudly as my friend's business went from strength to strength. I was happy at work and at home, I was earning good money, and had friends and a really lovely girlfriend who I was planning to marry until I came home one night, and Jo stood outside the front door with a rucksack. Before I could ask what she was doing, she kissed me and told me she loved me, then she put something in my hand, swung her rucksack onto her back, and left smoking a cigarette. She didn't even look back when I called to her.

The thing she had put in my hand was a note which read. I love you and That's why I want to set you free., Give it to the girl your heart needs. You'll find her right in front of your face. With love Joanne xxx Wrapped in the note was the engagement ring I gave her on her birthday. I drank an entire bottle of vodka and fell asleep face down on the living room floor.

I was woken up by a cup of coffee being slammed down on the coffee table. Jessie's voice rang in my ear. 'Get up Charlie you drunk, we have work to do, she's just a girl there will be others.'

When Jessie tells people she was a rubbish friend, that's crap, she stayed the night on my sofa to comfort me the night Jo left. Then she personally pushed my drunken backside to work the next day. Then for a while she would call me every day to make sure I was okay, and she arranged a work bonding trip to Alton Towers which she later admitted was partly to get me out socialising.

Anyway, skipping back to that night, I had not been looking forward to spending Christmas on my own, but things were looking up. I was learning to laugh again and that was all to do with Jessie, but the flowers were because I wanted to say thank you for everything. Jessie got a bigger bunch of flowers because I thought she would appreciate them more and look after them better. What happened in the moments before the train stopped was a bit of banter, but I got a bit uncomfortable when they joked about me wanting to ride on Jessie in the back of her car.

However, it wasn't really until Georgie said what she did, that I realised sometimes you can't see what's right in front of you. I just didn't know what I wanted, but Jessie prompted me to ask her out and I didn't know if she was teasing me. When I heard her calling and saw her standing there panting after chasing me down, I heard Jo's words in her note ringing in my ears. 'Give it to the girl your heart needs, you'll see her right in front of your face.'

When I saw Jessie coming towards me with her arms open, I realised it always had been her. All those summers and weekends hanging out in the park, and in the pub when we got older, I wasn't hanging out with her because she was with her brother. I was hanging out with Dave because he was hanging out with her. How stupid had I been all those years ago with all the noble not dating my best friend's sister crap. If I asked her out all those years ago, I wouldn't have been dating my best friend's sister, because Jessie was my best friend. But when I thought we were actually going to kiss, everything went to hell.

After the bump, I fell flat over on Jessie. She was my first priority. She was hurt, but not badly, but when we saw Tom's body in front of us, both of us were sick everywhere. The only time I'd ever seen a dead person was my old man in a hospital bed. My old man drank too much, but Tom was a young guy with his whole life ahead of him. Jessie was screaming as his blood poured over us and his head lay there looking up at us in the dark. Jessie was soon up and helping organise the evacuation of the train. It went by in a haze. I remember forcing the door open and helping people out of the train. I was lifting them down until the last few were gone. I think Kate was off first, because she was pregnant, and I may be wrong, but I remember Georgie only managed to put on one of her prosthetics.

But I will never forgive myself for letting Becky fall when she slipped, I just couldn't catch her, and the sound of her leg breaking as it hit the ground is something I never want to hear again. I don't remember who dragged her free, but I was worried. Jessie was still on the train, stood in the doorway looking down the row at the flames, calling for somebody who seemed to be still on the train. As I looked along the carriages, I saw somebody jump from the door on the far side covered in flames and roll onto the floor. I was certainly not an expert on train fires, and not planning on becoming one any time soon, but I was pretty sure diesel could explode at the right temperature. 'Jessie get out of there' I called, but she was still looking into the flames thinking there was somebody as she coughed and wheezed. I'd never in my life shouted at a woman, but needs must on these occasions. When is she going to listen?

I braved the heat and reached up, grabbing both her ankles, and yelled at the top of my voice, 'Jessica Louise Reynolds, get your stubborn backside off that fucking train before you get us both killed.' She turned to me with a sudden look of shock as she saw the flames, then she caught me off guard and jumped into my arms. Now I might be a big strong bloke and Jessie might be very skinny, but she's a tall lanky girl, bless her, and in catching her off balance she knocked me over backwards with a thud onto the grass. In a second, she was already apologising and pulling at me to get up, and we grabbed each other's hands and started after the others who had got a safe distance away. It was just like in the movies. We had run about thirty steps when there was a deafening bang and a feeling of lightness as we realised that the blast had thrown us off of our feet into the air.

We came crashing back to earth face down with a bump and I heard Jessie moan in pain. As we sat up in the darkness, I felt Jessie make a grab for me and she put her arms around me, breathing hard and crying with shock as I sat there in silence rubbing her back for several minutes. 'We have to go back,' she cried, 'Jimmy's still on the train.'

'No, we've got him,' I heard Mandy breathe in a panicked voice. 'Is everyone else okay?' Jessie and I both asked at once. 'No,' She panicked breathlessly. 'Becky has an open fracture. She needs an ambulance yesterday, Kate's just gone into labour, and Jimmy has caught fire and he's really very badly burnt.' I heard Jessie swear under her breath. 'There's more,' Mandy breathed, 'did you see John, Georgie, Jack, and Amber yet?' 'Yes, they got off,' we both shouted at once.

'They're not here.' she panicked, 'I saw them get off the train too but their all missing they're all missing.' At this point, Jessie stopped crying and found her voice. She was quietly spoken as always, so Mandy used her booming voice to relay her instructions as the remaining staff members congregated in the light from the burning train. She seemed really short of breath as though her asthma was beginning to kick off and a few times she turned and sneezed heavily but carried on talking to the group. Something I became aware of is that she had not looked at me once. However, her left arm was tightly squeezed around me, and she would not let go.

I tried to help her and Mandy communicate to the rest of the group as to what we were doing, but I was struggling myself. I began to realise that strangely it wasn't just Jessie who looked and sounded like she had the flu. Somehow all of the ladies in the group were looking unwell in the low light and several of them were coughing and sneezing. Even loudmouth Mandy was struggling to shout orders through her blocked nose until I gave her my pocket square from the pocket of my ruined blazer and told her not to give it back.

It was decided that Sue, who was a retired nurse and the oldest in the group was the best person to stay with the three casualties. The remaining fourteen of us split into two groups of three headed by Jessie and Mandy, to set off up the tracks in different directions and get help at whichever station was nearest, while two more groups of four would search either side of the tracks.

My hand went straight up to volunteer to lead the group to head south towards the river, but Jessie yanked my hand down and picked Sharon with Rob, Greg, and Michael, and then Mandy picked Chris, Ben, Cathy, and Rachel. Mandy, who was a short round lady then stood up to Sammy, who was the tallest woman I have ever seen, took a deep sniff, and said loudly and angrily in front of the whole group so everybody could hear.

'Sammy, you're drunk. Stay in front of me and we will be discussing your employment if we get back alive.' At this point, Sharon raised her hand quietly, and said, 'I'm a bit drunk too, am I fired?' Mandy didn't hear her, however. I quietly suggested that she put down the wine bottle in her hand and kept quiet.

Jessie, however, tapped Mandy on the shoulder and shook her head whispering something about Sammy into Mandy's ear who nodded, and her tone softened. I didn't ask her to tell me what she said, but we all had our suspicions about what was in Sammy's drink bottle. Jessie turned and quietly breathed into my ear that she was aware that Sammy was an Alcoholic and that she'd talked to Sammy who had agreed to go with her to an Alcoholics Anonymous meeting the following Tuesday. She had just reminded Mandy that we help our friends when they have problems and sacking her would be of no use to anyone.

The only problem with the plan was a young man called Greg. He hadn't been with us long and he quite loudly opposed the plan to search for people and said we should all sit and wait for the emergency services. 'And what do you propose we do about searching for our friends?' Mandy shrieked. 'They're probably in the pub. That's where I'd be,' he retorted. There was an angered response to his reply, with people booing. It was Kate who was lying on a coat propped up on a pile of briefcases holding her sister's hand, who spoke next, yelling breathlessly,

'My sister has a badly broken leg and could die from blood loss. My waters have just broken, the baby's coming, and my fiancé is missing and could be lying dead out there in the dark. How dare you accuse him of being in the pub, you little gobshite.' His reply sparked outrage as he said, 'I'd be in the pub if I was him.'

I felt Jessie grip my hand in anger. It was Mandy who shouted for calm and when she got it, she said firmly, 'I will give one thousand pounds to the first one to punch Gregory.' Several people stood forward, and there was laughter as the little weasel squealed and apologised to Kate, who quite rightly refused to accept it. We have all since said sorry to Greg, you will see why.

So, without a minute to lose, we left in our own directions with Spanish Sadie joining Mandy. That left myself and James to join Jessie who still had her head away from me and her hood covering her. We had taken off our winter coats and given them to Becky and Kate, and we found some other kind people had already soaked their coats in a puddle and laid them on poor old Jimmy who looked in a very bad way, and I hated to say it I was sure he would die.

Sue had tied every bandage in the team first aid kit around Becky's right leg which she had propped on a pile of clothes. By the look of her injury, she had a double open fracture above and below her knee, she was in so much pain she couldn't talk. I wasn't the biggest fan of her fashion, but she was a nice girl. I felt awful that from my inability to catch her, she would be lucky if the injury didn't put pay to her ambition of playing rugby for England ladies. Furthermore, I realised if we didn't get help ASAP, she could lose it like Georgie, or worse, she may well bleed out and die. Kate was already screaming as though her baby was coming and I saw Becky reach out and hold her sister's hand. After a very quick climb up to the track past the burning train, looking around and shouting the names of our friends to no avail, we turned right and headed east along the tracks back towards Yarmouth. I could see the lights of the Acle straight —the road that runs across the marsh, across the

fields from the railway. I was wearing my headlight. We only had one, as several people had left theirs on the train and lights had to be shared around. Jessie was holding me tight around my waist and even James grabbed my other arm, so we all knew where each other was.

James and I were shouting the names of our friends, but Jessie had pulled her woolly hat down and tied her scarf around her mouth, her head was bent towards the floor and her face was buried in one of her extra-large handkerchiefs as she breathed hard. When I asked her if she was okay, she shook her head and sobbed and that was when I realised, she was not just covering her face to avoid sneezing on me, but she had started to cry again and was hiding it. I didn't know what to say I just cuddled her into me as we walked. After a few minutes, something was bugging me, and I decided to come out with it and ask Jessie straight out why she pulled my hand down when I volunteered to lead the group that was going towards the river. I asked if she didn't trust me with leading. She didn't answer immediately, and I thought she was ignoring the question, then I heard her blowing her nose so she could speak. She spoke in a quiet muffled voice behind her handkerchief, saying, 'I trust you with my life Charlie, and I did choose you to lead.' Then, she turned her head to me and removed the handkerchief, saying, 'I chose you to lead this group.' When the light hit her, I jumped back in shock. The girl with her arm tightly around me with cuts on her face was not Jessica.

6

KATE 1

THIS IS A POEM I WROTE FOR MY JOHN TO PUT IN HIS CHRIST-MAS CARD AND I FELT I SHOULD PUBLISH IT HERE. A BLUNT AND HONEST POEM (SORRY I'M NO LINGUIST)

Before I met you, I was lonely and selfish, not without regrets.
I counted in my best friends, vodka, and cigarettes. (And not just the legal ones)
One day I turned up late for work still drunk from the night before,
Jessie put me with the new bloke, and I thought, 'Oh God, what a bore.
You were warm to me, I was rude to you, like turkey with cold gravy.
I picked on you for no reason. I must have driven you crazy.
Yet you to me were nothing but gold, just shut your mouth and did what you were told.
I threw a lot of shit at you, much more than most could hack.
Most newbies would have had enough by now, but you kept coming back.
And when you caught me snorting coke, you helped me through my rehab.
When I came out after three months, you took me for a kebab.
You asked me, 'Are you better now?' I smiled and told you maybe,
as months went by you stole my heart.
Now I'm pregnant with your baby.
Can't wait to live all the years to come, now you're to be Dad and I'm to be Mum.
I never thought someone could make me, as happy as you can.
As long as the Earth still turns, I will be your girl and you will be my man.
Merry Christmas, John, Love you always, Kate xxx

So, I'd used a bit of poetic licence there in the card it seemed he would never get, but I didn't know that then as I laid there contracting quicker than I thought I should be. I was worried that I was miscarrying our son as I lay there in the wet grass, sobbing my eyes out holding my sister's hand. I kept thinking to myself that this must be punishment for all the shit I did when I was using drugs.

I have to be honest, when Jessie talked about me being a pain in the backside in the early days, she was spot on. I was one of the people who was already working in sales when Jessie and Mandy started the company. They had previously joined the company I was working for, but they knew I wasn't happy and that's when they asked me to join their new company and I bit their hands off. They knew that I was a bit rough and ready, but I came with experience, they didn't know about my bad side then. They knew I smoked a lot and liked a drink, but what they didn't know is that I got into a bad crowd at school. I'd been smoking weed and drinking alcohol since I was about fifteen, but the harder drugs were a new thing. I tell a lie in the poem, as it was Jessie who caught me in the toilets at Norwich train station, and instead of reporting me to the police, she and Mandy helped me pay for rehab and kept my job open.

It was however my work partner John, who came to me every couple of days, telling me that despite the fact I was always being rude and mean to him, taking my anger out on him, stealing his money for cigarettes, and drugs, and basically being a diva all the time, he missed me and wanted me back at work.

He became my reason for not doing the things I used to, it was the hardest thing I ever did and it's hard even now, but I wanted to make John proud of me, as well as Jessie and Mandy. Rather than just give up the hard stuff, I pushed myself to go the whole way, with not only cocaine, but the other stuff too. When I came out, I'd also become teetotal and had stopped all forms of smoking. When I finally came out after three months, he picked me up in his car and took me to dinner. It wasn't actually a kebab, it was a well-known fast-food outlet, but Kebab rhymes with rehab. When I told John I wanted to make up for how I treated him, he talked about how he wanted to look after me and be there for me and get in the way of all temptation, and even wrap me up in cotton wool if it kept me away from the bad stuff.

The fact that my twin sister Becky worked for the company too, was nothing to do with me. It was pure coincidence that she was good friends with Jessie's brother Chris. It was hard that Becky and I didn't speak, yet we'd never had any arguments really. I suppose when using and for a while after, I just found her annoying with her bright-coloured clothing and her loud voice always running around. She looked like a clown and was an embarrassment. Really though, my feelings about Becky said more about me than her. I was an embarrassment for not accepting her for what she was. I wanted to make peace with her and be like we were before she came out, and before I hit self-destruct—the two things are not related. However, eating humble pie is not easy, and the right moment didn't come until we were forced together. I felt sick seeing my sister's leg so horribly broken, even though I was in a hell of a lot of pain, which was self-inflicted, and hers was not deserved in any way.

Sue (who was now seeing to Jim done a first-class job of bandaging her injury, but the blood was leaking through, I was scared for her life, but more importantly I was scared for her sporting career. I never told her how proud I was when I heard she had trials for England's women's rugby team, and she never knew that I went to watch her play in disguise, so I didn't distract her. However, that break in her leg looked so bad, she couldn't cry properly because it was hurting her too much and tears were just rolling down her face. At first, when I reached out my hand, she pulled hers away, but then just as I thought she was blanking me, she rubbed her eyes on her coat sleeve and smiled a little as she reached back and took my hand, and said with a nervous little laugh, 'Watch my gayness doesn't rub off on you.' I looked across at her, shocked and wanted to say something back to that statement, but I was hit by a huge contraction that took my breath away.

'JOHN WHERE ARE YOU?' I yelled into the darkness as I got my breath. 'H-he will c-come b-back, because he loves you,' I heard Becky whisper to me through her pain. 'But he wouldn't do this,' I told her, 'John would not ever leave, because he loves me no matter what I do, he isn't here, he must be....' But I didn't want to think of him dead or hurt.

'What's it like when he loves you?' Becky asked suddenly, squeezing my hand. I looked over at her shocked that she had even asked, 'So are the rumours true that you're sleeping with a certain larger-than-life redheaded lady?' Becky nodded and grimaced and cried out in pain as she was caught by a sneeze, then she said gently, 'It's friends with benefits, not love,' adding that it was an experimental thing to see if Mandy was really a lesbian and that they were not really a couple.

'Test her limits,' I grinned weakly, asking if Mandy ate toast. Becky shook her head and told me Mandy had stopped eating toast in favour of fruit salad, on her advice to try and drop some weight. 'Well, that in itself is a clue,' I smiled, telling her I was going to say nick a slice of toast but maybe a grape was better, 'If she gets in a grump, then maybe she's not the one, but if she is pretending to be angry, or play slaps you or even steals one back, that's very good.' I smiled as I told her all the things John let me get away with, all because he loved me, one example that morning when he offered to make me breakfast and coffee. 'I told him I didn't want any breakfast, but then his smelt so good that I ate it all while he was making coffee.' I saw a slight smile break on her pained face as I continued. 'He said nothing and as he turned to put more in the toaster, I drank his coffee, his only reaction to my naughtiness was to tickle my ribs give me a big kiss and ruffle my hair.'

John loved my little naughty moments. He said the fact I felt comfortable doing these things to him was a big turn-on. My list of little acts of naughtiness included waiting for him to run himself a bath and then jumping in it while he was on the toilet, shaving my legs with his razor, and taking his clothes to wear over my baby bump without asking. Most recently that evening I did the naughtiest thing yet, when I nicked his hanky out of his top pocket and blew my nose in it then put it back. Becky tried not to laugh when I told her this, but we were interrupted by another contraction. thankfully it wasn't strong enough to push, but it was hard enough for me to lose my breath.

'John, get your arse over here, NOW!' I screamed into the dark, but there was still nothing as Sue came and checked me over. 'You know this is the longest conversation we've had in three years,' Becky smiled uneasily. I teased that it was only because she was always rushing around, and I couldn't keep up with her. 'Well, I'll have to break my leg more often,' she said with a hint of sarcasm, before adding, 'Is this real, because you hate gay people?'

I was actually hurt by her accusation that I was homophobic. 'What have I done to make you think that sis?' I asked in a tone that sounded harsher than it was meant. 'It's because you don't like having a freak as a twin sister, isn't it?' She cried suddenly. 'You don't want me near your baby in case it turns out like me.' There were tears rolling down her face, but I was a little hurt by what she was implying. I would never keep my sister from her nephew or him from his aunty. She must have overheard something and taken it the wrong way. 'People told me the things you said about me,' she sobbed 'You said some horrible things about me. You said you couldn't stand being in the same room as me.' I was left cold by this, no wonder she barely spoke to me, I did not remember saying those things, but Becky was a lot of things, and a liar was not one of them. I must have said them before I got clean from the booze and the drugs, but if I had said something to people about her, it must have been taken out of context, but I'd grown up so much since I said those things.

'Becks, I'm sorry for....' 'Don't be,' She interrupted 'You only said what everyone else was thinking. I'm a twisted transvestite clown, who nobody understands. Just a joke. People don't know if I'm a woman or a man, and to be honest I don't know myself. I'd be embarrassed to be my own sister.' I sat there numb, I had always thought Becky was comfortable with what she was and didn't care what I thought.

'Becky,' I said quietly. 'Why would you care what some uptight washed-up drunken drug addict thinks of you, when you're a smart intelligent successful erm... Person.' 'Because...' she sniffed '...you're still my sister and my best friend even though we don't speak.' 'Well, we're speaking now' I said softly. 'Jealousy,' she said suddenly. 'What?' I sniffed as Becky wiped a tear. 'While you were screwing up your life, I was the brave golden girl who had the balls to come out. Rather than help, I revelled in the fact that I was the golden girl with all our family and ran you down and talked behind your back and said things just as bad as what you said about me.' She sniffed hard again and continued 'Now you've sorted yourself out and got a lovely man and a baby on the way you're the golden girl and I'm just that crazy half-woman half-man clown who did nothing to help you. 'What made you think I deserved your help,' I was saying when a figure suddenly walked into the light.

'John,' I shouted suddenly, it was my fiancé. 'John, where've you been all this time? I thought you were dead.' He turned sharply as if I'd made him jump from whatever world he was walking in. There were tears in his eyes and he had been wandering aimlessly when he looked at me, his eyes widened not with the usual look of love he gave me, but it seemed like fright, as though I'd done something to scare him.

He whispered, 'Kate? Beck? how can you be here? I've just watched you b-b-both die.' But before we could react, he had dropped to the ground between Becky and me, with the pair of us screaming.

7

CHRIS

I'm not going to go on about what happened in the build-up to the crash other than that somebody seemed to follow myself and Becky back through the town, but then disappeared when we got to Asda. That was when we saw Jessie and Mandy and played our joke on them which backfired, and I learnt many things from that, which I should have known. For example, my lovely little sister was twenty-three and very brave and a very talented athlete, and I was thirty-two and a bit of a fat fairy who stood no chance against her in a fight. Me and my sister Jessie get on so well and always have, especially seeing as she is nine years younger than I am, and four brothers came between us. When she was a kid, she was very clingy to our brother Dave, who was only three years older than her and his friend Charlie who she had a massive crush on. Our mum was paid as a childminder, but being the eldest child, a lot of the time I was the one who was keeping an eye on her customers along with my younger siblings.

Jessie was the only member of the family to stand up for me when I came out, and because of our family's reaction, she took my side and cut off all ties with our parents, which is something I did not ask her to do. Though to be fair Dave came around to the idea within hours and so did our other brothers. Our father was a nasty homophobe and mum stuck with him despite not sharing his opinion and Jessie punished both of them for that. I will never forget twelve-year-old Jessie throwing a whole pile of dinner plates at my father. Say my father due to the doubts that he was her father.

I thought as a big brother it was my job to look after my little sister, but she was the one who looked after me. Giving me a job in her company is just one of the ways she helped me out over the years. So, Becky was and is my best mate. It was very strange for a thirty-two-year-old man and a twenty-one-year-old woman to be best friends. I love her to death, but the fact that we met in a gay bar says it all. We have a lot of fun together, but there is no sexual attraction there at all.

Anyway, I've said I wouldn't go into the back story from the start, so I'll continue after the crash. Under Mandy's instructions, I was to head the group towards the A47 Acle straight, and instructions were to shine our lights on every blade of grass and shout for all we were worth to find our friends and colleagues while the others went off to get help or search the other side.

I took with me Ben, Cathy, and Rachel. There was a mix of ages there with Cathy the oldest of us, and Ben was youngest at Twenty-Five and Racheal who was either Twenty-Six or Twenty-Seven. I worried as we walked past the burning train what we would find. The missing people might be dead which was awful.

How would my poor little sister cope with the loss of her friends? Knowing her she would want to blame herself for putting those people in that situation, even though it was not her fault, and she was giving them employment. I tried to hug her as we split apart to search but she just clung to her friend Charlie, covering her face with one of her handkerchiefs, and didn't say a word to anyone, but instead dragged James and Charlie up the tracks as fast as she could, still keeping her face covered.

My friend Becky needed help, her leg was very badly broken, and I would have wanted to stay with her and help if the situation was different, but she had her twin sister to support her, even though they both barely spoke I was sure they cared about each other, but then we were also alarmed when Kate seemed to have a contraction.

Finding Kate's partner alive became the first thing on our minds as well of course as finding the other three missing persons. Ben, Cathy, Rachel, and I spread out, walking towards the road through the boggy field with a gap of about twenty metres between each of us. I didn't need Cathy or Rachel to shout to me where they were because both girls were coughing and sneezing in the smoke of the train. I became aware a lot of the girls were ill. In fact, all of them were and only a few of the guys. Our voices carried as we shouted across the marsh for Amber, Jack, Georgie, and John, but there was no answer from any of them. However, we were still in the light of the burning train when I heard the most blood-curdling scream and turned my torch to see Rachel falling to her knees. The rest of us came running over as fast as we could to her aid. She was on the floor with her head in her hands. In front of her was a melted briefcase and attached to it was a hand, and attached to the hand was an arm, and attached to the arm was a body burned so black that the face was gone, and it smelt like burned chicken. Nobody said a thing. We all saw the letters written on the briefcase JFG—our friend and colleague John Franklin Greymore, whose wife-to-be was giving birth to their first child only metres away.

8

—·—

MANDY 1

I don't like to beat about the bush. Obviously, my name is Mandy Brown, joint owner of JAM Enterprises, my best friend Jessie is the real brains behind the business, she was the Simon, and I was the Garfunkel, she was the brains, and I was the voice. (We didn't do the arguing bit)

Between Jessie and I we were earning a lot of money at the time, charging commission on sales made by our staff. Jessie was not in the business for money, but I was or at least to start off with it was all I cared about, but once I got to know people more, I came to care about the staff too.

To look at, I was short with red hair that went down to the point of my double chin. My big round belly was far smaller than it had been two or more years ago when I was morbidly obese but I was still very large.

When the train crashed, and our friends were missing I went towards Acle with Sammy and Sadie. We had our torches on and we were pushing ourselves so hard with the pace that I was out of breath and sweating, which is not hard when you're a big girl. The thing with me and Becky was a casual thing really. It started as a drunken one-night stand thing. She was doing her sympathy thing, saying how hard it was being a lesbian and finding other lesbians, let alone one who actually wanted to sleep with her or god forbid settle down. I was telling everyone how I was fat and ugly, and no man in the world had done anything bad enough to have me as their girlfriend. It was Georgie who had silenced everyone by suggesting that if Becky and I both wanted to sleep with people we should try sleeping with each other.

We all laughed at first, but I wasn't laughing the next morning when I woke up with Becky in my bed, I wasn't angry either. My reaction was more confused yet pleasantly surprised. People including Jessie had tried to persuade me that I might be since I was seventeen. It was just a strange drunken one-off, followed by another one, and another one. I'm not even that sure I liked her to start with, but she wouldn't go home, then I began to realise I did quite like it but wasn't quite sure how to move things on. I was being selfish in that it was Becky that I was thinking of more than the others.

I'd been playing her emotions unfairly, leading her on without telling her how I really felt and now she was laying there injured, relying on me. Anyway, in the chaos of the train crash, everyone was running around like headless chickens, apart from those who were hurt obviously. I was the one taking the register, and there were several people missing, even though I seemed to have seen everyone get off the train apart from Jessie, Charlie, and Jimmy.

We found Jimmy lying near the door where the fire had started, and he was so badly burned that I barely recognised him. My heart leapt when I found Jessie and Charlie lying on the ground, several moments after there'd been a massive explosion in which a lot of us thought they might have been killed. There were still others missing. Jessie looked like she was in major shock and was hiding her face from us all as she spoke deciding between us what we were going to do, if I didn't kill that little shit Greg for suggesting we all went to the pub.

Sammy and Sadie were with me and neither of them was my favourite person in the world, considering they had clearly both been in the pub despite doing quite well with their day's sales. Usually neither of them was in the mood to walk very quickly, but to be fair they did seem to realise the enormity of the situation and we were pushing the pace along the tracks. With only the light of our torches on the track, the dark open marshes stretched for miles on either side. We could not see the light of the Acle straight as it was very poorly lit, and that night there were no cars on it due to road works. I'd seen the spaces between the fields each morning on the train, and it was filled with ditches and dikes. I didn't envy Chris and his group, or Sharon and hers, searching the marsh for survivors.

I had this feeling that there may be people watching us out there in the darkness. It was like there were eyes watching us. You know how it is when you think you can feel someone's eyes on your back, and it sends tingles up your spine, but I said to myself as we walked that it was only cows or sheep, but then cows and sheep can be bloody scary. I kept imagining horrible things in my head like poor Kate giving birth to her baby in a cold field and it not surviving, or Becky's leg bleeding out, and where the hell were the others who were missing? Lord knows what happened to Georgie, Amber, Jack, and John. I'd seen them get off of the train but when the group came together, there was no sign of them at all.

Sammy was doing my head in too. A little of an hour into the walk, she kept walking at the side of the track down the bank from Sadie and myself, and when I asked her what she was doing it for she replied in her big Northern Irish accent. 'In case a train comes and runs us du fuck over, you silly woman.'

'You're the one being stupid,' Sadie told her bluntly, reminding her that it was a single track and that if there was another train coming the other way it would be at a station further up the line waiting for our train to pass it, and the signal would remain red until it did. 'And...' she added '...As our train is in a field back there, it's not going to happen.'

All of a sudden, Sammy screamed a piercing scream and we looked to the side to see her falling on her face. She was up on her knees quickly enough, and the three of us just stared at each other and the thing that had caused Sammy to fall. In the light of our torches, we all saw a girl lying beside the track badly injured. It was not one of the people we were looking for. She was blonde, but it was not our friend Amber. This was a big, tall woman.

'The lord only knows how this woman got here.' Sammy said suddenly making a cross on her chest. The woman looked up at us breathing sharply as though she was in a lot of pain and struggling to breathe. 'We need to help her,' I shouted to the others getting down on my knees. Sadie, however, shook her head at me and showed me her hands covered in blood from a deep stab wound in the lady's side. There was a pool of blood forming under her. A thousand reasons were forming in my head as to how she ended up out there in the dark.

Whatever this girl was doing here and whoever stabbed her, she was not long for this world. The situation was hopeless as I looked out into the blackness, all we could do for her as we wondered how she came to be there, was to hold her hand so she knew she was not dying alone. She stuttered and tried weakly to tell us something, but the language she used seemed to be something Sadie and I could not understand. Sammy however could well have been pretending she could understand to give the girl some comfort. Sammy listened with shock and fear spreading across her face, then all of a sudden, the woman sat up with a jolt and put her arms around Sammy and whispered in her ear before falling back to the ground where the poor woman took her last breath.

None of us knew what to say to each other. 'We need to get out of here,' Sammy said suddenly. 'What did she say to you?' I asked her with fear and adrenaline tingling down my spine. 'Let's just get gone,' she replied, standing up, having taken something from the woman's sock and her breast pocket. On her feet, Sammy started to work fast, leaving Sadie and I to run after her. 'What was she mumbling about?' Sadie asked her breathlessly.

'It wasn't mumbling, she was speaking Ulster Irish,' Sammy said breathlessly. 'In Norfolk?' I shrugged.

'Stranger things have happened,' she breathed adding that she was not the only person in Norfolk who was from Northern Ireland. When I told her it was strange that the woman had known she was from Northern Ireland, she went quiet. 'What did she say?' I repeated. Sammy stopped suddenly, and I saw tears rolling down her face. A look of fear appeared in her eyes like I'd never seen as she took out a cigarette and offered one to me and Sadie.

I was almost tempted having been a smoker myself until recently, but I pushed it away repeating the question. She took a sip from a bottle of Irish whiskey, which she seemed to have got from nowhere, 'I pulled the whiskey out of her sock and the cigarettes from her top pocket' she said quietly then continued. 'she said there are monsters out there in the dark. What killed her is coming for us if we don't move, it's probably already got Georgie, John, Amber, and that boy.'

'Jack' I added. She looked at me, shakily lighting up her cigarette as more tears fell down her face, and then she spoke louder in a warning. 'She said they're trying to raise the devil out there in the marsh and killing all witnesses.' She took a drag on her cigarette and sniffed before saying tearfully, 'I'm going to die.'

'Not if we run,' I told her, saying if we made a quick pace, we'd be off of the marshes soon and back in civilization where we could call the police, ambulance, and whoever we needed. 'It's too late for me!' she whimpered 'Not while you're still alive' I told her, dragging her arm as I started to walk fast, but she froze to the spot. 'I took the whiskey from her sock and cigarettes from her top pocket' she called in the dark.

'So, you robbed a dead girl, and you need to tell the police that, so you don't get yourself in the frame for her murder, but in the scale of things it's not that big,' I said going back to pull her along. 'Not a big thing!' she yelled staring at me and crying. She tapped her top pocket and her leg and glared at me. My blood ran cold as she told us, 'I keep my cigarettes in my top pocket, I hide Irish whiskey in my sock, because you're right, I am a fucking alcoholic. I have blonde hair and I speak fucking Ulster Gaelic.'

'What are you saying?' I quivered as her tone softened. I never saw anyone look so scared and confused as Sammy cried, 'I dunno how and I dunno, it seems impossible but that dead girl.... That dead girl was me.'

I stood there not sure if I should be angry at her for being silly and slowing us down, or if I should be very scared. I was definitely the latter of the two when all of a sudden something grabbed Sadie and took her from us before she had time to scream.

9

ROB 1

S o, I know what you're thinking, what was the great Rob Barn doing working for a sales company? What you're probably thinking is, who the hell is Rob Barn? People who were around in the early 2000s will remember a band from Lowestoft in Suffolk, who had a few global smash hits, they split up. Most people remember the name of the lead singer, but does anyone remember who the drummer or the bass player were? Well, that band was called The Darkness, and no I wasn't in it. However, my tale is one of how the mighty fall and my point is that nobody remembers the bass player. In my youth, I was the songwriter and bass player in a rock band called Rockcorn Storm, which consisted of me, three other lads, and a girl from my school.

Against all the odds we got signed with a record company, in the mid-eighties we were playing at Wembley Arena and crowds cheered and screamed, but that was usually about fifteen minutes after we left the stage, and the main act came out. We opened for some big acts at the time including Bonjovi, Bryan Adams, Meat Loaf and Queen to name but a few before our own single made it into the charts.

We were household names for a while, well for the four-week period that our rather mainstream debut single 'Love How You Rock' was in the charts. The music and lyrics were written by me, but all credit went to our lead singers Shane Sullivan and Lizzy Lambert (Real names Paul Samways and Clair Brook) because they had the voices and cooler names than Rob Barn.

They also had this fake story going on that they were a couple, but that was all media rubbish, and they didn't even really like each other a great deal. So, we had all the things we wanted, the fame, fans of both genders and the money. When we weren't touring in front of our own screaming fans, the guys were dating women who wouldn't have touched any of us with a barge pole if we weren't rich and famous, and Lizzy was sleeping with anything that moved. We could have made it really big, but instead of concentrating on the music, we enjoyed the lifestyle a little too much. After a short romance, I married a young model called Alicia from London, we could have been another big showbiz couple. We had money and fame. Alicia and I had just welcomed the arrival of our first daughter Gemma, when the band's second album was released.

Unfortunately, with the rush to keep us in the public eye and with distractions, the band's second album was written and produced with little care, and to be frank, it was not a classic and sales bombed. Within eighteen months we went from playing arenas to playing local theatres before the record company dropped us all together and we went our separate ways. I continued to work where I could playing guitar and singing in local pubs and so on, as well as running kids' discos, but I'm a musician not a singer and when the fame and the money goes, so does the attention of those who only wanted you for those things. My wife and kids were always more important to me than the fame and the money.

My wife however preferred the fame and the money and after a few more years of struggling to keep our marriage together, she applied for a divorce and cleaned me out, taking the house, the kids, and what was left of the money after some bad financial decisions. People see things in different ways I suppose, my ex-wife might say some stuff about me being a bad father, because I couldn't keep up her high-maintenance demands, or me calling her a cheating slut when she probably wasn't one at all.

The truth is I was down and out, and music wasn't making any money, and by the time 1996 came, I was doing odd agency work in Norwich. Why Norfolk when I was from Chelmsford? Because my ex-wife moved the kids up here to be closer to their grandparents meaning if I didn't move too, they'd be too far away. I suppose you couldn't blame a single mum of two for moving closer to her parents for backup, but I did because she should have stayed with me in the first place.

Anyway, that's how I ended up in Norwich. I met Mandy while I was working in Mcdonald's as a cleaner—yes, that was how bad it had got. I was emptying the bins when I walked past her out the back having a smoke, when she yelled, 'Oi, new bloke, weren't you the bass player in that band Rockcorn Storm?'

When I nodded, she stood there with her mouth open for about ten minutes before telling me her brother had been a huge fan at the height of our fame. Personally, she thought we were shit, and I couldn't argue.

That was when we struck up a friendship, it made me laugh that she knew who I was and respected my individual musical ability, while openly stating she had not been a fan of the band because the lead singer was a talentless gobshite. Rather than laughing at me, she had been somewhat sympathetic, seeing that I was struggling with the rent and paying maintenance money for the kids.

I think that was why she came to see me when she and Jessie started the company. She pitched it to me in this way in her booming voice.

'Tell people who you are, and they might remember you. Then you can give them your sob story of how you hit rock bottom and tell them you're now on your way back up and they will buy things from you. Oh, and remember to tell them what you're selling.'

She was right, knocking on people's doors and talking about the old days did sell more health insurance policies than talking about the policies did. It was a good thing that most people in the group were either too old or too young to remember me in my fifteen minutes of fame because that meant nobody took the piss about how the mighty fall.

To most people, I was just Rob, and that was just fine. I was doing okay for the first time in a long time, earning more than in McDonalds, making new friendships, and getting on well enough with my ex-wife that she was letting me have our girls for Christmas that year.

When the train crashed, it obviously took us all by surprise and we were all in shock. We were all running around like headless chickens. In hindsight, with a clear mind, I might have questioned Jessie and Mandy's decision to put Sharon in charge of one of the search parties when she had been drinking.

However, when there were more than twenty of us in the group, it is hard for everyone to know everyone, and Sharon was one of the people I didn't know so well. I knew Sharon to say hello to, but we'd not really had that much reason to speak to each other. I had heard that she had a reputation for spreading herself a bit thin or using her body to sell the health insurance we were all selling to dirty old men.

Basically, she wasn't my type of person from that reputation. I think we were all thunderstruck, not only because we were all bruised and shaken from the impact and the explosions and the fire, not to mention the dead body we had to step over. The only one of us without the blood of the poor train conductor on our shoes would have been that poor girl Georgie who didn't have any feet, but even she would have had it on her false feet. I heard that they never retrieved the conductor's body before the train went up in smoke. I suppose if somebody is already dead, then getting the living out alive matters more, and if that had been my son, I would have understood why nobody got him out.

I think what shocked us most is that there were people missing when we had all seen them get out alive, yet by the calling of the register they were gone. I think as the four of us, Sharon, Greg, Mike, and myself went off to search the marshes, we thought we would find the four missing people quite quickly because they had no reason to have gone far, if anywhere at all. This was even more so for Georgie seeing as she was only wearing one of her prosthetic legs when I saw her. One does wonder why any of them would have gone any further away from the train. In my heart, I hoped they hadn't gone back to help and got caught in the explosion, but it was my fear that I'd seen John headed that way. Sharon, despite what I'd heard about her was like a woman possessed as we began the search, any worries that I had about her ability to lead were answered when the moaning little upstart Greg tried to say he wasn't coming, and he was going to find a pub.

Before I could smack him one, Sharon had him by the ear like a mother in the Fifties disciplining a naughty child as she dragged him off into the dark. Mike and I exchanged rather frightened looks as we hurried after them not wanting to get on her bad side. After around 30 minutes there was nothing to show for our searching. We were sweeping a line with about Twenty metres between each of us shouting the names of the missing people. We stopped for a couple of minutes to check in with each other and to make sure we were all safe. As Sharon lit up what was somewhere between her third and seventh cigarette in the forty minutes or so since the train crashed, I saw tears of terror in her eyes. 'We need to go back the other way,' Greg was saying, and he added that if John, Amber, Jack, and Georgie had any sense they'd be in the pub.

'And what about John with his girlfriend going into labour? Should he go to the pub?' I asked angrily. His answer made me want to swing for him. He just calmly announced that if he was John he would be in the pub and probably take Kate with him. I had to hold Sharon back as she aimed a slap at him but ended up hitting me instead. The thing about Greg was that he sounded like an upper-class twit. The guy had intelligence, but he also had arrogance and often a lack of respect with it. That's how we perceived him on occasions, however having got to know him I realised that he's not that bad. He doesn't always realise that his intelligence works on a different level and something that's obvious to him is not always so to other people. We were just as guilty for not listening to him. People thought he was being obnoxious and uncaring by saying these things. If he had pointed out what he saw as obvious a little earlier, things would have turned out differently.

As Sharon apologised for hitting me, Greg just looked at us both quietly then said calmly, 'There's a pub on the road about a mile or so from the train or actually it could be a diner I've seen on the bend in the road.'

In anger at his further comment about the pub, Sharon grabbed him by the collar and drew her hand back to wallop him. However, she stopped dead and lowered her hand without taking her gaze off of Greg, but her angry look changed as we all had a sudden epiphany. Either Greg really was an unfeeling asshole, or we should all have been paying more attention to him, including the others in the team who had gone in their own directions. After a moment's silence, it was Sharon who spoke not taking her eyes off of Greg. 'There's a phone in the pub and none of us listened to him,' she breathed. 'He wasn't being a shit.' She added, 'He wasn't talking about going for a drink. He was pointing out the obvious and we should have listened to him.'

Sharon pulled Greg towards her and kissed him on the cheek. As she did so he pulled a rather disgusted face as though the thought of her touching him was repulsive—in hindsight, it may have been because her breath was full of smoke. After she pecked him on the cheek, she then slapped him quite hard on the very same spot, saying that it was for not making himself clear enough earlier. Following that rather heated moment, the four of us closed in together so we could all hear each other speak and there was a heated, but friendly discussion, regarding whether or not we should abandon our orders to search that area, and go to the pub.

I remembered now having driven along the Acle straight in the past, that there is a tight bend in it as it almost reaches the railway. On that bend was the pub or Diner Greg was talking about. It's no longer a pub or diner since it's conversion to a Hindu Temple of all things.

Chris and his group were already headed in the direction of the road, but they were heading north and might not think to go for the pub once they got to the road. Jessie, Charlie, and James were walking east toward Great Yarmouth, but they were following the tracks. They would pass within a few hundred metres of the pub, but probably not see it from the tracks. We thought the pub was north-east of the train, and neither of those groups would hit the pub directly. We'd been searching for a while and with no sign of the missing people it may be a better bet for us to aim straight at the pub. For all we knew the missing people may well have been found already.

We all agreed that we should abandon our search and go to the pub, and we started to walk back heading east of the light from the burning train so that we met with the road closer to the pub. We trudged back towards the tracks at a breathless pace following Sharon who despite not being in peak fitness had found an extra gear and was almost running across the dark muddy fields, never mind the fact the place was crisscrossed with dikes full of cold water. I tried to explain to her that we didn't want to be falling in the water as hypothermia was the last thing we needed to be dealing with. We'd been walking for about fifteen minutes when Mike stopped dead. He was just stood there talking to himself and looking from the now dimming light from the train to our left, and then to the lights of Yarmouth to our right, then to our very far left where we could not see Acle at all.

Very far to our right along the line there was a very faint light, which I hoped and prayed was Jessie and her group making progress towards Yarmouth. 'What's the hold-up?' Sharon was demanding to know as she came stomping back. 'The train is almost dead centre of the marsh,' he said not looking at us.

'That's great,' Sharon snapped. 'Now we know that, can we get going to the pub please?' 'But That's just it,' he breathed. 'We're going the wrong way!' 'What?' Sharon demanded. 'If the train had gone around the bend,' he breathed hard, 'We would see Acle on our left, but not Yarmouth on our right.' Sharon and I and Greg all looked at each other as if to say, 'Shit He's right!' The pub was on the bend and the lighting on the Acle Straight was and still is very poor, and remember it was also closed for repairs, but if Mike's theory was right, we should have headed northwest as opposed to northeast as we had been. It was Mandy's party that would be missing the pub by a few hundred metres and not Jessie.

No matter which way it was we needed to get there quickly because with the road shut the pub would be too and we would have to break in.

Another idea that hit me was that if the road was being worked on, there'd be workmen with transport to get us to help. Looking up and down the unlit stretch where I knew the road to be, it worried me that there didn't seem to be any work at all going on there. In fact, I wondered why they had even bothered closing it. We'd been walking less than a minute when Mike suddenly tripped and fell. My first fear was that he had fallen into a dyke. However, he was on his feet again in seconds and had picked up whatever caused him to trip. It was a cloth, it was covered in mud, but in the light, it seemed somewhat familiar, like I'd seen it before. Sharon shrieked in shock as she saw it in the light. 'That's one of those pocket squares Georgie made.' 'Of course!' I thought to myself, Georgie was a lovely kind lady and one of her many hobbies was embroidery, and earlier in the year she'd given every member of the team a gift of a personalised pocket square. 'Whose is it?' Sharon demanded as Mike tried to unfold it.

In the light of my head torch, I saw the initials J.L.R 'Jessica Louise Renalds' Sharon breathed. We all stared at each other. We all saw Jessie walk up the tracks with Charlie. There was no way her pocket square could have made it out to as far as we were unless something had happened to her. Greg suggested half-heartedly that it might have blown on the wind. However, the wind was very light and there was no way that could have happened, plus I could still make out the very faint light far off in the distance making progress along the track. When Sharon suggested that Jessie may have given the pocket square to somebody else, we all began to shout again for our missing friends as we continued towards the pub with our hearts racing with panic.

Greg was the next person to fall, and he screamed like a girl. If not for the seriousness of the situation I may have laughed, but I realised why Greg had screamed and I was almost sick. In the light of my headlamp, I could see that Greg had tripped over a female leg, which had been detached from its body.

All sorts of things were running through my mind as to how a leg got to be there so many miles from anywhere. Sharon however just picked up the leg and gazed at it like a woman possessed. 'You mad woman, that someone's leg,' I told her in disgust. 'Exactly,' she smiled 'It's not a real leg, it's one of Georgie's prosthetic legs which means...'

'It means Georgie's been here,' Greg added. 'Or Amber,' Sharon finished. According to Sharon, Amber had been carrying one of Georgie's two false legs when they got off the train as it seemed one of them wouldn't fit. Just as with the pocket square, nothing could explain what it was doing there. Neither Georgie, Amber nor anyone had had reason to go anywhere, let alone this far from the train. As Sharon and I both reached down to help Greg to his feet, the pair of us slipped and fell to the floor ourselves, knocking Mike down with us. After much swearing, we all managed to sit ourselves up in time for another shock. When we looked up, we were surrounded by a ring of bright light that pierced the darkness and it scared us so much that we grabbed each other in fright. The ring of light came from twenty or so flaming torches. The twenty torches were held by people all wearing dark and terrifying masks.

10

JESSICA 2

So now we come to my second piece. I would like to start my second stint of writing in the hope that this is all making some sort of sense as we switch between each other's positions to keep the story in the correct time scale. I would like to apologise if the end of Charlie's bit was a little misleading because he's only male. I have given him a small kick for doing that. Only joking. I say this in jest of course because he's such a lovely guy. As it has been mentioned we are all here together writing our story in the pub, and he's here with me now and he's just been to the shop up the road and bought me a big net of satsumas and made me a big cup of coffee, love him. I may not have mentioned that I'm currently very pregnant with my third baby and my two-year-old son George is sitting here, sleepily watching CBeebies on my iPad.

Anyway, the strange girl clinging to Charlie, hiding her face was in fact me. When Charlie saw me, however, he jumped to the wrong conclusion and asked, 'Who are you and what have you done with my Jessie?'

This is the problem with men—I tease—jumping to all sorts of conclusions when all that had really happened is I had taken off my glasses because they were smashed in the blast. I'd been hiding my face because I wanted to get walking and didn't want to waste any time fixing the injury to my face, which I was hiding under my handkerchief.

I think it looked worse than it was, but I didn't want time wasted on me when we had friends out there missing, and Charlie would have wanted to stop and do first aid on me. Unfortunately, the cut was caused by my glasses smashing in the blast when the train exploded, which may I add was the scariest thing in my life up until that moment. (Apart from childbirth)

Any plans of sitting at home watching TV the next day were going to have to be replaced by dragging my flu-ridden backside to the optician. More's the fact I would actually need some kind friend to take me there as I couldn't see. When Charlie realised what'd happened, he joked that I should have gone to Specsavers and got a spare pair. When I told him I had done, and he asked me if I'd brought my spare pair, I had the humiliation of telling him that they were my spares, because I broke my very expensive designer pair when I slipped on the ice a week earlier and didn't tell him in- case he worried about me.

So that's why I had asked Charlie to lead, I was embarrassed to admit that I couldn't see a bloody thing. Charlie was good about it. He told me how brave I was to have gone charging out into the night. 'Well, I can't sit around and not help while our friends could be dying,' was my retort, 'Plus, it's my fault we're here in the first place.'

I went on to tell them how it was me that had spoken to the clients whom we were selling the health insurance plans for and arranged to work in Great Yarmouth for a week and a half. As I explained to James how the business worked knowing that Charlie knew the ins and outs of it. I explained how we were given a list of places to canvas and a time scale, then Mandy and I made the decision on where to go and when and told everyone else the week before. We had been due to canvas Ipswich, but I was too exhausted to drive my Mini full of people and stuff, and then walk miles. I wasn't going to make my staff pay for the train to Suffolk, so we'd settled for Great Yarmouth only to find the Acle straight—the road across the marsh—was closed for repairs for two weeks and we had to either drive around, or get the train, and due to timing and cheaper tickets, the train had seemed the best option.

Charlie was silent. Unable to see, I felt somebody touch my back and feel under my blazer jacket. I shrieked a little but calmed when James told me it was him. I'd have slapped him if he hadn't said the sweetest thing when I asked him why he'd done it.

'Well.' he laughed, 'With all the hard physical and mental work, and things you do for the company just so we can have jobs and income, I thought you might be hiding your Wonder Woman costume under there because that's what everyone calls you behind your back.' I went red with embarrassment at such a compliment, and I asked Charlie if he had paid him to say it and told James that kind of flattery could earn him Employee of the Month.

We didn't have an Employee of the Month because we value everyone the same. 'You two are such a lovely couple,' James added. James had joined after Jo had left Charlie. 'We're not a couple,' Charlie told him. 'I've known Jessie for twenty years,' he continued adding, 'I asked her out earlier and she said no, but we still love each other as friends, right, Jessie?' 'I didn't say no,' I told him firmly. 'You didn't?' 'No, Charlie,' I said quietly, thinking back now to the moment when Mandy's joke had made him walk away. 'Before that horrible joke, which Becky is very sorry for,' I told him, 'I was trying to say I want to stay home in the warm tomorrow and blow this cold out of my nose so we can have fun when I'm well enough to go out.

'And,' I smiled, 'I was rather hoping you'd like to come over and make hot drinks and switch the videos over and pass the tissues.' 'If we make it out of here...' he said squeezing my hand. '...the first thing I am doing with you is getting you some new glasses, and then I'll make the drinks, change the videos, and pass the tissues.'

'Becky was actually quite funny' He added tightening his grip on me. 'It was like something big sis Sarah would say to me.'

'Bless her' I nodded.

'Who's Sarah?' James enquired.

'My old neighbour and Jessie's brother's girlfriend,' Charlie told him for me, 'Sadly both no longer with us.'

'I'm sorry I didn't know!' James said putting a hand on my shoulder.

For a long time, we just walked without saying a word to each other about what happened. The cold wind was battering us from what seemed like all sides, stinging my face as I struggled a little to breathe. Charlie had insisted on taking my bag because I'd walked a lot further than he had earlier in the day.

I didn't protest as I was struggling with a pain in my side where he had landed on me when we fell. None of us wanted to speak about what happened on the train, or the horrors we'd seen.

Like Dave and Sarah, Tom was dead and most likely so was the train driver, none of us knew either of them well, but still. Surely they had families who were expecting them to come home. Tom was just a nice young boy with his whole life ahead of him, it was just so unfair that he died like that. I knew what it was like to be the one receiving the horrible news. Seeing Tom's head brought back horrifying thoughts of what happened to my brother and lovely Sarah. They had both been decapitated and squashed so hard that Sarah's heart was in Dave's chest.

I couldn't think of that now. My concern now was for those who were missing and doing all we could to stop them from joining the list of dead. Jack, Amber, and Georgie were all seen getting off the train, yet none of them were there when Mandy called their names. Those three would not have disappeared without good reason. John too, there was no way on earth he would have left Kate unless something had happened to him. Charlie kept checking our mobile phones every few minutes to see if we could get a signal to alert the emergency services. Our nineties mobile phones were rather primitive compared to those we have now in the twenty-first century, and they were certainly not as common as they are today. Their batteries lasted forever because there wasn't colour, let alone internet for Google Maps and apps. The network coverage in most areas of Norfolk was poor, I thought it may be better out in the open, but there was nothing. We'd been walking in a straight line towards Yarmouth for about forty minutes before James nervously spoke.

'We should've been nearly there by now.' He was right, we were all in quite good physical shape. I had one of those step counters which people used to measure exercise in the days before smart phones and Strava. I used it to check roughly how far I walked when working. I passed it to Charlie who read it aloud, telling me that we'd walked just over two and a half miles in Forty-Eight minutes. 'That's not fast enough,' I panicked, 'We need to pick up the pace guys!' In hindsight, it was probably the shock of the situation that was clouding my judgement. I was a fit girl. I'd pride myself on regularly completing up to four miles in an hour and swam lengths of the pool with Georgie three mornings a week. I was angry at myself for being so slow and didn't want to hear it when Charlie told me it was not my fault that I was ill. Instead, however, I rudely told him to be quiet and save it, then I started jogging until James spoke over both of us and said 'Look, guys, this marsh is eight miles across. If we were halfway across and we'd covered nearly three miles, then we've only got one more to go, but if we were more than halfway across, then the other group had less to walk and they're probably already in Acle getting help. That's if the train company haven't already sent a search party.' 'Yeah, what he said,' Charlie added breathlessly. I wasn't listening. I blamed myself. It was my decision to put twenty people on the train when we could easily have gone in cars despite the Acle straight being closed.

My head was banging, my throat and face were stinging, my nose was dripping, and I was streaming in sweat, but stupidly I ignored the wheezing and tightness in my chest. I pushed on hysterically, despite Charlie asking if we could at least slow down for a sip of water. I couldn't see where I was going, but as long as I could feel the track bed under my feet, we were going the right way.

All of a sudden, my breathing difficulties took a turn for the worse. I stopped dead, but I couldn't catch my breath. It was like I was breathing, but there was no oxygen getting to my body and my head was spinning. I remember looking up at Charlie in the torchlight as I crumpled to my knees in pain. I heard James in the background panicking, saying, 'Charlie, what in the hell is happening to her?' Then in my panic, I heard Charlie's voice say, 'I think Jessie is having a massive asthma attack!' For a moment everything was black, even the limited vision I had was gone, but I felt something in my mouth, and I took a sharp breath and felt a cold misty spray.

'Slow breathing, Jessie, keep it calm.' It wasn't Charlie's voice I could hear, but it was a soft warm male voice at my side, and several figures came into my vision and my heart pounded as my lungs screamed. Charlie, love him, was kneeling holding my inhaler with the massive spacer connected. He must have seen me do it enough times to figure it out, but the voice I could hear was not his. It belonged to a young man on my left-hand side who seemed to have his own source of light. There was a girl as well to my left-hand side. She was young, blonde, and very pretty, and I thought for a moment we had found Jack and Amber, but it was not them. The young man had dark spiky hair, and the small blond woman had a large birthmark on the left side of her face. It could only be them.

Concentrating hard on my breathing, I couldn't speak, but just looked on with confused love into the faces of my big brother, Dave, and his lovely girlfriend, Sarah, as their ghosts smiled at me. 'Hang on in there, little sis, you nearly died then, but you'll be ok with Charlie here!' Dave smiled. His familiar voice was a whisper on the wind. I couldn't take my mouth from the inhaler to speak as I felt Charlie give me a second puff, but I heard my own voice whisper, 'I miss you guys.'

'We're always here keeping an eye on our loved ones,' Sarah told me with a smile. 'What's heaven like?' I heard myself ask. 'Couldn't you tell we went to hell?' Dave smiled jokingly. 'For us it's love for each other with motorbikes and pubs,' Sarah smiled 'But you're not invited until you're at least Eighty,' Dave added.

'You need to listen quickly sweetheart,' Sarah told me. Dave continued smiling, 'We are so proud of you for everything you've achieved, but this tonight was no accident. All your friends are alive and safe for now, but there's something big going on. We don't know what, but it isn't good and there are many people out here tonight other than your friends.' I tried to listen, but the ghosts were already fading as I got the Ventolin into my body. I heard Dave rushing his words to me as he was fading. I caught him saying something along the lines of telling me not to make up with our parents until they apologise to Chris and me, but maybe not even then. The last thing I heard him say was 'For God's sake, hurry up and kiss Charlie!' They were gone and Charlie's out-of-focus face was all I could see. I felt his warm hand supporting my back and pulling my hair out of my face as he spoke gently.

'Well done Jessie,' he was saying. 'Keep it calm, sweetheart.' Still a little way from comfortable, I took control of the inhaler myself, trying to smile at Charlie with my eyes, and then reached out with my other arm and snuggled Charlie into me until I could breathe. Charlie and I just looked at each other for a moment, even though I couldn't see much. He took something else out of my handbag and I felt him put one of my clean hankies in my hand. I thanked him weakly, and he rubbed my shoulders as I sat there giving my nose a thorough clear out. When I was finished blowing my nose, without saying a word, I pulled him towards me as we sat there and slipped our tongues into each other's mouths. We totally forgot what we were doing there, for what could have been a hundred years. All those years of wanting and never getting, loving, and never quite telling, wishing he would love me back, and being too blind to see he already did. It was even better than I could ever have imagined, and I could have spent the rest of my life on the cold tracks kissing my man. However, when we finally pulled apart both Charlie and I both seemed to have forgotten why we were there. He reached down and took out his flask and poured a cup of coffee and passed it to me.

We sat down with our legs out, our feet against the tracks. Leaning our backs on each other we passed the coffee to each other and talked about our surprise at having kissed after all these years. I was still trembling badly, but wasn't sure if it was from the kiss, or the Ventolin coursing through me. I haven't had an attack like that in a long time.

'Why on earth did we not do that before?' Charlie breathed as I sipped the coffee. 'You being engaged to my friend until a few months ago might have been part of the reason.' I teased, still in shock.

'Sorry about that.' he said nervously. I told him not to be sorry about it, because he loved her. 'I did,' he said quietly, adding, 'I loved you first and always have, but I'm not fit to lick your boots.'

'You can lick them if you want.' I smirked trying not to giggle as I reminded him, we'd been in a field and my fake fur boots were probably smeared in cow shit. I sneezed twice more and sat for a moment blowing my nose with a big honk, and then took the cup of steaming coffee from Charlie and had another sip.

'Charlie,' I said bluntly, passing the coffee back to him. 'I always knew you loved me, but I always thought it was like a brother loves a little sister he wasn't able to have, but if you had feelings, why didn't you say? and did you really think you weren't good enough?' Thinking back, I'd learned a lot of the things I was good at from Charlie.

It was him who taught me to swim and ride a bike as a child. It was he who showed me the ropes at my first job. He even gave me driving lessons, even though it wasn't legal because he was only nineteen.

'It wasn't the done thing to start a relationship with your best friend's sibling.' I nodded and thought about it for a second while I sipped more coffee. He was right. When we were kids, relationships with your best friend's siblings weren't the done thing, and probably still aren't. I thought I'd twist the situation and make him laugh, so as I passed the coffee, I teased him.

'I fully agree with that statement.' I laughed. 'There's no way I'd let you be in a relationship with any of my brothers.' I heard him spray the coffee through his teeth, laughing as I shuffled my bottom back. I turned to face him, then I put my arms around him and snuggled my head into his shoulder. I clung to him for warmth, and I felt his arms around me tightly as the cold wind blew my long hair in all directions.

'Is that your way of saying you were my best friend?' he asked softly in my ear as we rubbed each other in an effort to keep warm. 'Did you only hang out with my brothers because I did?' I asked bluntly. 'Not to start with,' he replied running his fingers in my hair, 'Of course Dave was my friend but you were just as much of a friend if not more at times.'

'And the fact that my mum was paid as your childminder until you were at high school?' I laughed pulling his leg. 'You want to know how long I've had a crush on you?'

I sniffed rubbing my seemingly ever-dripping nose with my hanky. He nodded. I asked him if he remembered the time when I was twelve and he was fourteen and I was home from school on my own in bed with an asthma flair-up and was hooked up to my nebuliser. My mum was working and my dad was out, and he skipped school and bought me chocolates and a get-well card.

'The days when a simple box of chocolates could make you feel so much better! he nodded. 'Well, my crush on you started years earlier!' I laughed quite honestly. 'I ate the chocolates and threw up, and you took the blame,' he reminisced. 'You still owe me another box.' I teased playfully.

'Do you remember that time your mum thought we were having sex and came storming into your bedroom?' He laughed hugging me tighter.

'We were just jumping up and down on my bed because you were excited because you beat me at chess for the first time.' I smiled adding that at the time I had no idea what sex was, giggling incoherently.

My giggling got worse when Charlie told me there was a rumour suggesting that I still didn't know what sex was. I just smiled and informed him regretfully that the existence of my virginity was only wishful thinking on my part, after a horrible first relationship which I ended after only a few weeks. That was followed by two other short-lived crap relationships.

'So,' he said softly, 'These must be the only circumstances where a smart business-woman like you, who earns three times what I do, gets together with an employee and it might last if we're lucky.'

'Three things, Charlie,' I told him. 'One, I already told you you're Mandy's employee. Two, this relationship absolutely will last, and three...' I paused and blew my nose (Yet again) while I figured out how to tell Charlie that as part owner, I actually earned 12 times what he did in a year. That was why I often bought everyone food because I felt guilty about making so much money. The contractors set the payment rules, not me! When I told him he just laughed and said he regretted turning down the third partnership which Mandy and I offered him when we first started our company.

'Though,' I told him, still not breathing right, 'I would give all the money in my bank account and more for another kiss.' I felt him lift his head and he whispered gently in my ear, 'You can have this one for free.' With that, he took me back to heaven for a good few minutes. 'So, here's the question,' Charlie asked, once I'd finished attending to my runny nose again. 'What do I call you now?' I had a little think about it.

'Boss lady' I giggled. 'You're not my boss, remember?' he teased. 'Okay, well just call me Jessica, like always,' I smiled. 'I never call you Jessica,' he insisted. Until I reminded him that he had shouted my full name at me when I wouldn't get off the train. 'THE TRAIN,' we both shouted.

What on earth were we doing sitting there kissing when our friends were missing? I could've shouted at Charlie for not reminding me what we were supposed to be doing, but strangely he was just as annoyed at himself for somehow forgetting. Clearly, we both got caught up in the moment, and just couldn't help ourselves, but if it was anyone's fault it was mine for pushing myself into the asthma attack. I couldn't push myself now, my chest was still tight and my breathing was still fast and shallow, my heart rate was still tachycardic.

Basically, for those of you who don't realise how serious asthma can be, there was already a chance I could be ending the night in the hospital myself if I made it that far.

I had to take the rest of the walk very steadily in the hope that our little stop wouldn't put our friends in further danger.

'Hang on,' Charlie said as we were about to get walking, 'Wasn't there someone else?' Suddenly I remembered, screaming, 'Where's James?' My heart racing, we searched up and down about Fifty metres of track where we'd been sitting.

There were tears in my eyes as I shouted for James, and I could hear Charlie calling for him, but then suddenly I heard nothing. I turned back up the tracks, now looking for Charlie and shouting his name, but there was no sign of him at all. However, it could just have been that my eyesight was so bad.

Dave and Sarah's words were still ringing in my head as I called out for Charlie and for James. 'There are many people out there! Something big is going on! Everyone is alive for now!' All I know is that Charlie would never leave me.

Obviously, he's safe now as he wrote part of this book, but in that moment, I was suddenly more alone than ever. I didn't know whether to go looking for them or turn back to the train where I wouldn't be alone but would have let down my friends. Or should I keep going towards the town before whatever was hiding in the dark came back for me.

My sight was terrible. Looking either way I could see the faint light of what I thought was the burning train, just a dot behind me, and the lights of the town seemed no nearer to me than they had been before, but that could have been because my eyes were so bad. Tears were streaming down my face and my heart was pounding with fear. I thought it best to keep walking towards the town with my head down, not looking either way, not wanting to see what was there in the dark even with my sight impaired so I wouldn't see it anyway. I had only been going minutes when I looked up ahead of me.

To my relief there were two figures with torches walking quickly towards me. Thank my lucky stars it must have been them coming back for me. I was all ready to slap and kiss the pair of them for leaving me there, but as I put my arms out blindly, I grabbed the nearest person in a hug, it was the shocked voice of Sadie who spoke. 'Jessie, how the hell did you get here?' Then, I heard Mandy's voice say. 'What the actual fuck is going on?' All sorts of things were going through my mind as to how on Earth they came to be there, and I was sure they were not expecting to see me either because both of them just stopped.

Without thinking about the entire madness of the situation, the first words that came out of my mouth were 'Where's Sammy?'

'She went with another group,' said a strange but familiar male voice, who went on to ask how on Earth I managed to be there all alone when I went off the other way with

Sophie and Jack. 'What? Who's Sophie?' I asked, now so confused that I was not sure if the whole of this was some cruel dream.

'Jack, Amber, John, and Georgie, are all missing, remember?' I told them, adding that Becky and Jimmy were badly hurt, and Kate was in labour, and now Charlie and James are gone too.

'What are you on about? You must have hit your thick head' Mandy replied forcefully, and what she said next made my blood run cold. 'The train derailed. You went for help to Yarmouth with Jack and Sophie. We came this way, Cathy, Greg, Mike, and Sammy went to search the marshes. Chris, Ben, Rachel, and James went towards the road. That leaves Charlie, Rob, Sharon, John and Maggy missing.

'No That's wrong,' I repeated 'There's nobody called Sophie in our group, or Maggy! Jack, Amber, Georgie, John, Charlie, and James are missing. Becky and Jimmy are hurt, and Kate is giving birth. How did you get here?' I asked repeated getting quite angry with Mandy for the first time ever in my life.

'What are you talking about Jessie?' she replied, with more concern than anger, 'I don't know anyone called Amber, Jimmy, or Georgie. Sue is badly burned; Becky is not hurt, and Kate will not be giving birth any time soon.'

'Who what where are you talking about?' I asked bewildered as I heard Sadie burst into tears. It was the male voice who spoke in a soft whisper, 'Becky and Kate are both dead and "YOU" climbed over their dead bodies to save yourself you bitch.' I think my heart actually stopped beating for a long while.

I couldn't believe it and grabbed the young man for support. I thought I was going to faint. I caught my arm around his neck, and he grabbed me by the shoulders calmly. 'Get lost, you nearly took my head off you selfish cow!' 'he said not so gently as though he was mad at me too.

Looking at him from closer up, I could see his face better, but it was still blurry in the dark without my glasses. It had been one thing seeing the ghost of my long-dead brother and sister-in-law-to-be while I was almost passed out.

I was alert now and ghosts were not real, but they had to be, because when I saw him, I screamed harder than I had ever screamed in my life. The last time I saw that face was an hour or more ago, looking up at me from a pool of blood from the floor of the train, not attached to a body. I must've been dreaming. Tom could not be here when I'd already watched him lose his head.

11

— ◆ —

SUMMERY BY JESSICA

So, at this point, several people have had their say and written the first part of what happened to them. We have all been here together at the pub putting our story together. Even some of the people who haven't written their own pieces are here to corroborate stories as it's not worth several people writing the same thing. Becky and Sharon are just two examples of many people here who have not written in this volume but may well continue their stories in the next volume. However, with all these people having a story to tell, you can't write a long story all in one day, so that's why we've had to break it up into pieces, given that we've all got homes to go to, jobs to do and kids to feed. So, having got this far, I just want to summarise everything that we know so far in case you've missed something or misunderstood. Firstly, when the train derailed, we counted everyone off apart from Jimmy who had tried to fight the flames and somehow managed to get himself out at the other end, however, he was badly burned.

Georgie, Amber, Jack, and John had all disappeared after getting off the train. Some people said they had seen John running back to the train, and I certainly thought I saw somebody else on the train helping Jimmy as Charlie was screaming at me to get down.

Last we heard; Amber had been dragged off into the dark by a terrifying monster. This was seen by Georgie who had given chase as well as she could with one leg being plastic, but she'd fallen and knocked herself out. Georgie herself has told how she had spoken to a young medium earlier that day, who had warned her she was in danger and that the key to her survival was Amber. That turned out to be Amber the person, and not the colour of a key, it was Amber who saved Georgie's life when she was trapped and drowning in cold coffee. Georgie was now lying unconscious and unfound in the dark marsh. Nobody had seen or heard from Jack. Rob, Mike, Greg, and Sharon had searched the marsh, then tried to find the pub, but got lost and then found the hanky/ pocket square that I gave to Amber when she was crying and one of Georgie's false legs. Then they themselves were captured by some strange people in scary masks. Mandy, Sadie, and Sammy had gone towards Acle where they were surprised to find a dying girl lying on the tracks, and to their horror, it was Sammy herself. (Yes, I know it seems wrong and twisted).

Then Sadie had been snatched from thin air. Kate and Becky had stayed near the train with Jimmy who was badly burned, and Sue who was looking after them all. Kate was having huge contractions while the break in Becky's leg was the most horrible injury I have seen in my whole life. Chris, Ben, Cathy, and Rachel searched the roadside of the tracks where they found John's burnt body. Charlie, James, and I had gone towards Yarmouth, where I had an asthma attack and saw the ghosts of my brother and his girlfriend, and I kissed Charlie as you were just reading. Then on coming to our senses, we realised that James was missing. Then shortly after that Charlie vanished too leaving me alone until I somehow found myself facing Mandy and Sadie.

You may have missed these vital and worrying things.

1) Sammy saw herself die, which was not hard to miss.

2) After Sadie was taken, that left Mandy with Sammy, but when I found her miles from where she should have been, Mandy was with Sadie, and Sammy was missing. That left the question as to who the people I found really were, and why and how Tom's head had somehow found its way back onto his shoulders.

12

— • —

JENNY 1

Hello, I am Jenny. You're now wracking your brains to remember when you heard Jessie mention Jenny on the train. Well, she didn't, so now the mystery deepens until you reach back into your brain trying to think where you've heard of me in this story, and then suddenly you remember.

If you haven't got it by now, I'm the strange creepy girl who showed Georgie I could read her past. The truth is I've always had this ability. I'm a medium far greater than Doris Stokes or any of these people you see on TV. I will not judge them, because even though a lot of them are frauds doing it for fame, they give people hope.

Hope is something I rarely got the chance to give people. I do what I can. Unfortunately, I'm not of the belief that my powers had been given to me by God, because they were not. My powers go far beyond talking to the dead. I'm human, but I am not like any human you probably know. I suppose if you knew about my people you would call us warlocks, witches or even mutants. I was born into a dark bloodline. It goes much deeper than I can explain. Since the dawn of mankind, my people have been hiding in shadows doing the work of Satan, bringing death and destruction to the average man. There were always very few of my people, but they were responsible for some of the greatest atrocities in the history of planet Earth. It's a long and complicated story, but the basic outline of what I know is that at the beginning of humanity, the force known to you as the devil saw the Earth thriving. This displeased him or her and for some reason of deep jealousy, the devil created my people with the power to bring it crashing down and planted us among the human race to destroy it.

However, the force which created the planet through millions of years of evolution, (known as God as well as many other names, wasn't happy and sent its own magical humanoids to defend the planet from my people. As a good friend of mine called Sally once put it, 'God and the devil were busy fighting each other and forgot about us.' For thousands of years my people have fought a long-standing battle, with my people trying to destroy the planet and eradicate the defenders while they tried to get rid of us.

The battle came to the attention of mankind in the 1600s with all sorts of people being accused of witchcraft and killed in the cruellest of ways for the most stupid of reasons. Only two of those killed were real witches, two sisters in a small Norfolk village. They were the last of the defenders. Their deaths should have paved the way for my people to take the world in our own hands and destroy it all.

That however did not happen, obviously, because we're all still here. The last act of those dying ladies was to do something that prevented our magic from directly killing anyone. With our powers unable to do what had been given them for, my people retreated into the shadows where we stayed until such time when something could be done to break the spell. In hiding now, they couldn't kill people outright. My people used their magic to make the human race inflict death upon itself.

A few of the more recent things include two world wars, and multiple terrorist attacks, including 9/11 in New York and the 7/7 attacks in London. All terrorist organisations, Isis, Al-Qaeda, the British and US governments to name just a few, and many more, all have my people behind them. Obviously, those things hadn't happened yet, but my people continue to do these things to this day. Getting rid of people with disabilities by cutting their benefits and forcing them to kill themselves, while using the money they saved to drop bombs on other countries.

I might have liked that idea if I was on their side. Of course, in life we make choices, and they affect our life and the lives of those around us, but there are some things we cannot choose, like to whom you are born. I was born what I was, and my abilities were seen as 'special' even to my kind.

So you might ask yourself if I'm so bad, if I really am evil, why am I exposing it and how come to Jessie and Mandy and the rest of these lovely people have let me tell my story in their book? Well for one, nobody will take me seriously, but the main reason is that although I Can't choose not to have my evil instincts, I can choose not to act on them.

My powers are so strong that the voices of the dead reached me before I could talk, but they were not the voices of my people. They were the voices of the ghosts of those dead witches who gave their lives to protect the human race four hundred years earlier. Certain laws of magic regarding secrets prevented me from hearing some of the things they told me.

Despite this what they said helped me to make my choice not to act on my evil instincts. Think of me as a vampire who refuses to drink blood or a werewolf who locks themself in a cage before the full moon.

I told Georgie all she needed to know at the time and of course, it wasn't all strictly true. I was not the little girl I first appeared to Georgie as. That was a disguise to fool my grandmother just like the curse I put on her to give the evil cow dementia in her old age. Georgie said she thought I looked older when I stood in the doorway. I'd just turned nineteen but had morphed into a twelve-year-old. A trick that fooled even my own mother or so I thought.

My relatives thought I was what they call a null, a person born into a family of warlocks who has no magic. I was hidden away from the world, a forgotten child. You'll find no record of me on any birth certificate, or schooling, which meant no social life and no friends. I was just a slave to my family, or so they thought.

While my family slept, I would walk the streets of the town, some nights I would break into the pleasure beach and climb to the top of the roller coaster and listen to the voices of the townsfolk in my head.

What I heard was not just the voices that come from the mouth, but those that come from the soul. That's how I felt Georgie coming that night, it was not just her. I heard Jessie worrying about her staff, always wanting the best for them. Kate and John radiated love, but there was something not quite right about their love which I couldn't quite grasp.

That poor girl Amber with the pain in her heart and the desire to kill herself from two miles away. All of them were visitors to my town and their voices stood out among the usual voices in my head. I felt I knew these people and I knew they were in danger. That's why I told Georgie to go straight home. Georgie however didn't listen, and I don't blame her. She would look very strange telling everyone to go home early because some crazy girl told them they were in danger. If you remember Jessie said in the prologue that she could hear somebody sneezing behind them.

There was something following them through the darkness of the old town, something dangerous and frightening lurking in the shadows.

It was me, just like the rest of the ladies who are writing, I had a horrible cold, but the main deference was that I knew why everyone was ill. My people were doing something out on the marsh that black night. I heard whispers, not just people talking, but thoughts in their heads, talk of awful things such as raising the devil himself.

I didn't believe they really had the power to do that, but in any case, it was scary stuff. It was a potion they were creating for their get together on the marsh that night. It was the fumes that were making people ill. For an unknown reason it was only females who were getting ill from it. That's why they were sneezing and blowing their noses poor loves. The potion was being made all over town. It was being made in different homes where my people lived including my nanna's. That was how all of the ladies working for J&M got ill, having been in a lot of houses that afternoon. It was why Georgie's cold got so much worse when she was visiting my nanna and me.

Symptoms were very similar to the flu, or a very heavy cold. Many people had colds because it was winter, so the effects of the potion were being masked. So shortly after my meeting with Georgie, I told my Nanna I was off to bed. Rather than go to sleep, I locked the door and jumped out of the bedroom window. This didn't hurt half as much as you may think, because between you and me I can fly.

Flying is not something you should do in front of everyday people if you don't want yourself to be exposed. So, I followed on foot, watching the guys and girls as they went about their work and then I followed Jessie and Mandy as they made their way to the train. As I say, I didn't know the plans and I thought talk of raising the devil was just talk. I just wanted to make sure that these innocent people got home safely.

So, after following them in the shadows, I sat and watched them for a while as they waited for the train. The more I watched them, the more I realised how much I craved to be normal. These people were all friends. For the most part they had no ill feelings toward each other. They helped each other and shared things like food, drink, and cigarettes. They looked after each other like a big family, and here was me on the outside looking in, wanting to be part of it all. I could feel pain radiating from Amber as she sat sobbing at the end of the platform. I wanted to go and tell her that everything was going to be fine, but however much I thought I knew her, she didn't know me at all.

I was glad when Jessie found her there and got her to calm down. I could also hear Georgie wondering loudly in her own mind about things I told her as she sat with the others, not really listening to a word they said but doing a good job of pretending. When the roaring diesel-burning monster of a train rattled out of the darkness I watched as they all got on to the front of the two carriages. When they were all aboard, I shot like a flash out of the shadows and took my place behind Jessie.

What Sharon saw thinking she was drunk, was the flash of me, zooming across the platform to the train. I'd never been on a train before, so it was all new to me. In fact, this was the first time in my whole life I'd gone outside of Great Yarmouth. I sat there listening in to all of the voices in my head coming from all the people on board. All I had wanted to do was make sure these people got back to Norwich safely.

I planned to return to Yarmouth with the train on the next service. There was no plan for me to show myself to anyone there. I just wanted to make sure they were safe as the train passed by whatever horrible shit my people were up to on the marsh. At the same time, I hoped I may hear some of the voices in my head telling me what exactly it was that my people were really doing out there. As I've said, it was really unlikely that they were actually going to raise Satan.

However, if my powers could be of any use to keep the train safe, I wanted to be there to do what I could. I was not expecting the number of voices in my head to increase in the way it did. There were suddenly thousands of people talking all at once, not talking with their mouths, but with their hearts and souls. These were not the dead who often contacted me, these were the people out on the marsh.

This was much bigger than I expected, there must have been enough people out there hiding in the dark to fill Wembley Stadium. My head was screaming when the bump came all of a sudden. In the darkness I could hear cries vocally in my ears, drowning out the many voices in my head. I lay on the floor, unseen by the other people as I tried desperately to untune my psychic link to the people outside the train. By the time I really came out of the trance, I found myself almost alone. Most people had left the train and it was already burning. I could see Jessica stood at one end of the train looking down the aisle with Charlie pulling at her to get off.

At the other end I saw Jimmy with a fire extinguisher, trying in vain to put out the flames. A normal person's instincts would have been to run for the exit.

However, as I've said, I am not a normal person, and being fireproof is one of my many powers. So, my instinct was to run through the flames surrounding Jim and get him out.

When Jessie shouted to Charlie that she could see somebody in the flames it was me. When I got to Jimmy, he was already on fire. As I grabbed him and dragged him towards the far exit, engulfed in flames, I felt a strong voice in my head. 'You're not meant to save him,' it said loudly. I ignored it. No voice in my head tells me who I can or can't save. I may have been born bad, but I do not let people die. 'Let him die,' it repeated clearly. I continued towards the door, which opened for me without me touching it. As I lowered him on the step, I saw pain and fear in the old man's eyes as he dropped and at that moment, I knew I'd done wrong.

It was his soul that spoke to me as he rolled, and it said hauntingly. 'It was my time. You've robbed me of my death.' I was still stood there in a moment of shock and realisation that he had intended to die; the train exploded and took me with it. I think you may be wondering how on earth I'm still alive to tell the tale. There's one problem regarding me pretending to my own people that I don't have magic. If you don't have powers, but you know about them, they become a closed door. A person who doesn't have powers, but knows about their existence, cannot be allowed to tell the wider community about it. For this reason, people born without magic are not allowed to know any details about how to use it.

If this was Harry Potter, for example, a person born to a wizarding family who was not a wizard, would not be allowed to go to Hogwarts. Remember as I've told you, my people are the bad guys, and that's why I chose to hide my abilities from them.

So, after not being taught anything about my powers, I had to teach myself things when I could. Most of it came from using my extraordinary hearing to eves drop on lessons from afar, but I far from knew it all. So when the train blew up, that was the end of me, right?

Well, obviously not, because I'm here writing this without so much as a scratch on me. Well, apparently, I can't die, at least not in that way. I was blown what must have been about fifty feet into the air and fell to the ground with a thud and searing pain like I had never felt. I remember landing on the tracks and seeing blood pouring out of me, my right leg was gone and so was my left arm and there were fleshy balloon-like things hanging out of my chest. I soon realised they were my lungs. Surely I was a goner. All I had to do was lie there and wait for the devil's minions to drag me off to hell where all my people go.

They don't let my people into heaven. I've never been so scared. I was a traitor to my people, many of whom would be welcomed in hell as dark angels, but not me. I was going to burn forever. I remember everything going black as though I was asleep, but then woke up as though it had all been a dream.

There was no pain, my arms and legs were re attached and my lungs were back in my chest where they belonged. I thought it was all a dream and that I'd woken in my bed. However, unless my bedroom was on a railway track and the rails were my bed, which obviously was not the case, then it was all true, and my powers had put my broken body back together.

For a moment I just laid there dazed with the noise all going on around me. I looked to my right, and I saw what was left of the train burning, the roof and windows were gone and there were seats scattered around it, also burning and melted. The smell of burning plastic, metal, and oil, filled my lungs, causing me to choke. My first instinct was to fly away, just because I can fly. I will add that I didn't want people to find out about the extent of my powers then, and that's why I didn't just fly straight to the town to get help. You may think, why expose my powers in a book while not using them to help people? The reason that I feel it's okay to write about my powers while not using them to help people is this.

If I write about them while using a false name, you can't trace me, and you can choose to believe me or dismiss the whole story as fantasy. If however I was seen using my powers, for example, reporting the crash two seconds after it happened by flying to the town, I'd be exposed. Captured, locked up, and taken for testing. When I lifted off into the air to get a better look, it was in the cover of smoke. Looking down I saw not one, but two trains burning on either side of the single line, one on my left and one much further along to my right on the opposite side of the track a few miles towards Great Yarmouth. How could it be that two trains were travelling on a single line? Had they collided head-on and then somehow spun away from the track in different directions on either side of the embanked track? No, they were too far away from each other for that to happen.

My first thought was anger. How on earth the railway company could have let two trains onto the single track I did not know. My limited knowledge of how railways work tells me that trains using a single-track line should be held in sidings and passing places to let each other past. The service from Norwich should have crossed our train many miles further up the line and there was no service scheduled for earlier. It was unlikely that it was a charter train for a private party, and even so, it would still have been held, so the question remained, what the hell were two trains doing on the track and how was I still alive? However, as I say, the trains were too far apart to have hit each other.

Strangely after I'd been there a few minutes, I started to see people from both trains organizing search and rescue parties.

It seemed that somehow over a few minutes, the trains somehow seemed to have got even further apart. I couldn't see the road below me at all, in fact, it seemed to have gone altogether. On both sides of the track, I could see hundreds of tents pitched, far enough away to not be seen from the train. There were lots of other things out there, I couldn't see what they were without light, but it all looked terrifying. The layout of the land below was almost as though there was a symmetrical pattern, as though somebody had cut up two maps down the line of the railway, and then stuck the two halves together the opposite way round.

All these things were put to the back of my mind when I looked straight ahead and saw something that made my blood run cold. Hovering way above the earth, brushing herself down and cackling, with a cruel smile beaming over her face as she looked at the chaos and destruction all around, was someone I knew all too well. It was a person I saw an image of every day, but who couldn't possibly be flying above those train wrecks. There was only one type of place I ever saw that person, and the reason she should not be there is because that place was the bathroom mirror. I had just come face to face with myself, only it was clear to me that my other self did not share my views on using her powers for evil, and by the look on her face, as she flew at me, she'd been expecting me.

I had only heard of such things in old folk tales that I overheard my people telling each other. When an act of great evil causes a rift in time and space in which two or more dimensions collide with each other causing people to cross into each other's worlds. Something had shaken the very fabric of reality.

Whatever happened next, we were all in deep, deep shit.

Continued in Volume 2 The evil in the darkness.

Out Now

Printed in Great Britain
by Amazon